The Crystal Eye

THE CRYSTAL EYE

Anecdote
Publishing House
For the love of quality reading!

Anecdote
Publishing House
For the love of quality reading!

anecdotepublishinghouse.com
champreaders.com

Anecdote Publishing House
2nd Floor 2/15 Lane no. 2 Ansari Road, Daryaganj-110002
Email: info@anecdotepublishinghouse.com
Website: anecdotepublishinghouse.com

Published by Anecdote Publishing House

First Edition 2025
ISBN 978-81-982589-8-4
MRP ₹ 350/-

Book Promoted and Marketed by Champ Readers Pvt. Ltd.
Book edited by:- The Book Bakers
Cover design by:- The Book Bakers
Layout by:- Arivazhagi Balasundaram
Printed in India

CHARACTERS

Nirmala:	Daughter of priest, Sita Kund
Binod:	Son of an engineer, studious
Rakesh:	Hails from a lawyer family, strong built
Prasad:	Father of Rakesh, a prominent lawyer
Shakti:	Son of a priest at Kashtaharni Ghat temple
Dubey:	Shakti's father, a priest at Kashtaharni Ghat temple
Rupa:	Shakti's father, a priest at Kashtaharni Ghat temple
Vinita:	Mother of Rakesh, a housewife
Ramu:	Peon of Prasad
Bhim:	Gardener at Rakesh's house
Vikram:	Dreaded criminal from Bardah
Ramesh:	Constable at Munger police station
Kim Davy:	Russian criminal

ACKNOWLEDGEMENTS

गुरुर्ब्रह्मा गुरुर्विष्णुः गुरुर्देवो महेश्वरः ।
गुरुरेव परंब्रह्म तस्मै श्रीगुरवे नमः ॥

First and foremost, I thank God for providing me with the strength, inspiration, and perseverance to complete this book. To my family, your unwavering support and love have been my anchor throughout this journey. Your belief in me has been a constant source of motivation.

To my friends, thank you for your encouragement, understanding, and for always being there to lift my spirits. Your companionship has been invaluable.

To my readers, your enthusiasm and feedback have been the driving force behind this work. I am deeply grateful for your support and for embarking on this journey with me.

To my publisher, gratitude for providing a platform to let my imagination reach a wider audience.

Lastly, I extend my heartfelt thanks to my book agent, Suhail Mathur of The Book Bakers, whose guidance, expertise, and dedication have been instrumental in bringing this book to life. Your faith in my vision has made all the difference.

TABLE OF CONTENTS

Chapter 1

Aeons ago, Shankar and his Nightmares

Aeons ago...somewhere in Mithila...

Shankar woke up in the middle of the night sweating profusely. Cool breeze of the summer night blowing steadily through the open window had failed to calm his anxieties. First few times, when he was still a fourteen-year-old kid, he used to wake up crying and take refuge in his mother's lap to calm himself down. But that was almost a decade back. He was all grown up now. Although the nightmares still scared him, he knew there was no point in waking up his mother. There was nothing anyone could do. He lit the fire torch, opened the door quietly, took his walking stick and started walking on the unpaved road. It took him almost half an hour to reach the Shiva temple a mile away at the outskirts of the village.

This had become his schedule whenever he had the nightmare. The first few times, his mother used to calm him down. But, he always felt bad waking her up in the middle of the night. He had been a Shiva disciple since his childhood.

After one such nightmare, he felt like going to the Shiva temple. He really felt at peace there. The temple did not have a door. In the wee hours, the Shivalinga appeared almost mystical. He would sleep on the temple floor. When his parents couldn't find him at home, the villagers, would join in searching for Shankar, only to find him at the Shiva temple sleeping peacefully.

Soon this became the usual ritual. Whenever he had a nightmare, he would slip away to the Shiva temple, meditate for some time and doze off. The temple priest would come and wake him up the next day.

Shankar was born premature. He had a slight hump on his back and his left leg was slightly deformed. He had a difficult childhood. Kids used to stay away from him because of his hump and bent leg, but his parents always stood by him.

"You are different because you are a special one, Shankar. You are a gifted one. Look at the sign on your upper right arm," his mother would say proudly.

His mother was an expert in herbal medicines and commanded immense respect in the village. Shankar revered her. He would look at the sign on his right arm. The birth mark of an eye was exactly the same as the one his mother had. No one in the village had it. When anyone mocked him for his physical inabilities, he would look at the eye on his arm and feel better.

His physical limitations kept him away from the kids and people in general. What does a child do when he is alone? Shankar started thinking why he and his mother had this particular birthmark. He would go to the nearby Shiva temple and keep thinking about it for hours trying to find an answer. Slowly, the eye became an obsession.

One night, Shankar was exhausted from helping his father on the farm. They had spent the entire day tilling the land and preparing the soil for the next planting season. Despite his physical limitations, he never shied away from hard work, and he truly enjoyed seeing their efforts bear fruit in the form of crops in the following season. After the harvest, they would head to the market together to sell their produce, which sustained them until the next planting season. His body would throb with the strain of the day's toil.

A tired mind is vulnerable, especially to obsessive desires. In his dream, he saw a pitch-dark tunnel. The darkness, combined with eerie silence, made him sweat even in sleep. In the faint light, he saw six strongly built men escorting a godly figure. The men were armed with all kinds of weapons, while the godly figure appeared to be a lady with a glowing body. The men were escorting the lady away from a tunnel and into a temple. The temple had one crematorium each on its East and West sides, making it appear as if death surrounded it.

On their way out of the tunnel, they bowed in front of a large Shivalinga. As they left, he could see the beautiful Shivalinga more clearly. It was almost six feet in height and had lot of snakes wrapped around it. There was a faint light emanating from it. Shankar could see a wheel with seven spokes carved on the Shivalinga. Suddenly, the Shivalinga came closer. He saw that each spoke on the wheel had the same eye as he and his mother had on their arms. The Shivalinga kept coming closer, its light emanating from it blazed like a blinding fire. The blaze engulfed him and he woke up, drenched in sweat.

"Mother, why did the fire engulf me?" Shankar used to ask the first few times he had the nightmare. His mother did not have an answer. Initially, he experienced these nightmares almost weekly. However, as he grew older, they became less frequent. He still felt scared at times, but as he grew, the frequency started decreasing. He used to get scared even now, but he had found a way to calm himself meditating at the Shiva temple.

His obsession with the eye grew so strong that almost all day, he started thinking about his birthmark and why both he and his mother had it.

It is said that our subconscious is very powerful. It helps us in becoming and achieving what we desire. And it turned true for Shankar too, three years later.

❁ ❁ ❁

Chapter 2

Three Years Later

Since early morning, the villagers had been preparing for the festival of colors, Holi. Amidst the revelry of the festive celebration, a group of youngsters had taken the intoxicating bhang (cannabis), that too rather liberally. When one is not in control of one's senses, the evil in oneself is generally more dominating. They saw the crippled Shankar walking alone towards the Shiva temple. There were few people around, but they were busy and a band of villagers was playing drums loudly, making it hard to differentiate between revelry and a fight.

"Hey you cripple! Where are you going? Come here! We have some medicine which will straighten you up!" teased a naughty kid from the group.

Another grabbed his hand.

"Let me go! I am going to the temple," Shankar shouted.

"Look at his arm, friends. The fiery eye is watching us! Be careful! Who knows Shiva might be watching through this eye," one of the guys mocked.

"Don't you make fun of me! I have not done anything to you. Let me go." Shankar tried in vain to pull his hand away. But the grip tightened. When he tried to use his walking stick to stave off, another guy snatched his stick. Then two more pounced on him. The festival of Holi is such that it is natural that people come closer, hug each other while throwing colors and enjoying themselves. No one nearby sensed anything foul. They dragged him away where there was no one to watch and started beating him mercilessly. A few punches landed on his hump. Shankar shrieked in pain. A blow landed on his forehead. He sat down holding his head. They kept kicking him till he fell on the ground. Shankar was motionless. The gang got scared.

"Is he dead? What are we going to do now?" Shankar's left eye was swollen. His face was covered in blood and barely recognizable. One of the guys kicked him to see if he was alive.

"Water…please give me some water," cried Shankar in a feeble voice. There was no water. One of the guys fed him bhang from the leather pouch he was carrying. Although Shankar never liked bhang, he took a few sips in order to moisten his throat.

"Let us leave this place now. We will be in trouble if anyone sees us."

While Shankar lay motionless, the gang quickly ran away from the place leaving Shankar behind, almost dead on the ground.

It was almost four hours before someone noticed him. "Who is this guy? What has happened to him?"

A small crowd assembled around him. "It looks like Shankar. Look at the hump on his back!" One person ran to bring some water and wiped Shankar's face with his cloth. His eyelids opened up, only to close soon. Lips opened up slightly but no voice could be heard. As soon as the word reached his parents, they came running.

Shankar's mother cleaned his wounds. "How can people be so merciless? What has the poor soul done that he suffers so much?" his mother started crying. His father brought some hot water in a bowl. His mother put some herbs in the water and extracted its juice. "Ah, be careful!" Shankar would scream whenever his mother applied the herbs to his wounds.

"Don't worry my child. You will get well soon," said his mother.

"The concussion on the head looks really bad," said his mother to his father. "It will take a long time to heal. The strong herbs would put him to sleep for some time so that he gains some strength." She was still crying unable to understand how people could be so brutal.

"Please do not beat me. Leave me alone," Shankar screamed late evening. His mother came running towards him. "There is no one here, dear." She held his hand and softly touched his head to calm him down. He was sweating profusely. She opened up the door to let more air come through. She gave him some more herbs that she had prepared. He quickly fell asleep.

"Please save me. I am burning. Mother, I don't want to die." He woke up screaming in the middle of the night. His parents came running to him. His mother again gave him some herbs and put him to sleep.

From that night, the frequency of his nightmares started increasing. Unlike once a month or so earlier, he would now get it almost every other night.

"It looks like the concussion has had a deep impact on his head. God knows when he will get better!" his mother said with a sad face to his father.

"We will consult the village physician tomorrow," said his father.

With the first light of the next day, his father called in the village physician. Although Shankar's mother was also an expert with herbs, the village physician was almost ninety years old and had vast experience.

"What has the society turned to these days? Shankar is such a humble boy. I have never seen him troubling anyone. Such violence! It looks like the boys didn't spare a single bone!" said the village physician.

"His nightmares have also become more intense Guru ji," said his mother.

"Hmm, it is because of the blow to his head. His wound is deep. That is why he seems to have lost control over himself and his nightmares have increased both in frequency and intensity. You both need to take extra care of him. I am giving him some more medicines. I honestly don't know how long he will take to recover. Our prayers are with him," said the physician before leaving.

❁ ❁ ❁

Chapter 3
The Vision!

Almost a fortnight later, Shankar regained some strength. He was able to walk with the help of his stick. One night when he was sleeping, he had a slightly different dream. The Shivalinga was the same, but instead of the six men escorting the lady out of the tunnel, he saw six men and the same lady meditating in front of the Shivalinga. Just above the wheel, on the Shivalinga with seven spokes, he saw a crystal. It was this from which a faint light was emanating. The intensity of the light soon increased multi-fold and he saw all seven people becoming stronger.

The seven people then came out from the tunnel, went into a river, and proceeded to a temple nearby. They went inside the sanctum sanctorum. When they bowed down, Shankar could see the idol of Chandi.

Although the dream this time was slightly different, the ending was a lot different. It did not end up in the blaze engulfing Shankar!

And then the nightmares that used to trouble him almost daily since the beating, stopped suddenly. His parents were happy though that the nightmares had stopped. He did not tell parents that the last dream was slightly different from the earlier ones. Now that Shankar was confined to his house, he had even more time to think about his dreams.

"There is definitely a reason why I am seeing these. My birthmark also matches the eye on the Shivalinga. Probably, it wants to say something to me through these dreams," Shankar thought.

***

In the backyard of his house, he found a large copper plate. It was thin and almost the size of his window. He found a chisel and a hammer and started engraving the Shivalinga onto it.

"What are you doing Shankar?" his mother asked, worried that he had not fully recovered and might stress himself more, despite this, his father allowed him to keep doing. Otherwise, there was hardly anything inside the house that he could do, and they didn't want him to go out yet.

Over the next four days, Shankar completed his work. The copper plate had a Shivalinga engraved on it. Like in his dream, it had a wheel with seven spokes. Each spoke had an eye formed on it, identical to his birthmark. A crystal was placed on it, emitting a few rays. A short distance away, a temple was engraved on it—the same temple he had seen in his last dream. Inside it, he carved an image of Chandi.

"What have you made Shankar," his father asked one day as Shankar was deep in thought, staring at the copper plate.

He didn't answer. Now that he had the details engraved, he was more confident of not losing details of his dreams. *But what was the mystery of the Shivalinga? Why did it bother him only? Was he really the only one having those nightmares?*

The light had definitely made the seven people meditating in front of it stronger. Did the Shivalinga really exist? Shankar's mind felt like it was overrun by ants, a chaotic invasion of relentless thoughts.

His father was a farmer. Shankar had only been to the nearby market a few times to sell crops with him. His mother used to fetch herbs from the jungle on the nearby hilltop. Shankar had gone with her very few times since it was difficult for him to walk on the steep incline. He would slow down his mother and they would not get much time to search for the herbs, pluck them and return before it was dark.

Should he take help of someone? But if the dream was true, it may excite others also to explore. He was not ready to share his vision with anyone at this point of time. And after all, he had not seen anyone else having the birthmark that he and his mother had.

"Is really a secret somewhere calling for me or is my mind just playing tricks with me." He would often think. One day, he asked, "Mother, like I got this birthmark from you, did your parents also have the same birthmark?"

"My dear son, only my father had this mark," replied his mother going back into her memories. My grandfather had died before my mother's marriage and she was very attached to him. "Your grandfather was the pride of the village. He was the strongest of the men. Once, a leopard had entered the village in the night. It was pitch dark except for light of the fire torch the night guard was carrying on patrol. He ran away shouting for help. When your grandfather heard him scream, he went out. My mother didn't allow me to go. But villagers said that he showed a lot of bravery in the way he tied up the leopard to a rope. The villagers then put him inside a cage and left it deep inside the jungle".

"Did you also see anyone else having this mark, mother," asked Shankar.

"No dear, since my childhood, I have not seen anyone having this mark. Your grandfather used to say that I was lucky to have this. It made me more beautiful. I never saw it in the village I grew up in, and in this village, too, I haven't seen anyone with such a birthmark," said his mother.

Shankar was hesitant to ask about his last dream. He didn't want to trouble her mother again unnecessarily. He hid the copper plate in the backyard. His parents knew about it. But many people used to come to his mother for various treatments. What if it aroused anyone's suspicion?

A few days later, he went to the Shiva temple at the outskirts of the village.

"How are you, Shankar? It has been a long time since you came here," enquired the priest.

"Purohit ji, I have recovered well now. It has been quite some time. I really feel at calm at this temple," said Shankar.

"True, I missed you. You sit here. I will come in a little while to talk with you and bring some prasad as well," said the priest.

Shankar nodded and sat at his usual place. The priest returned after some time with a delicious looking sweet. He sat near Shankar and said, "You are a very kind hearted person, Shankar. I am glad to see you recovering fast. I also heard that your nightmares have finally stopped. You have Shiva's blessings my son. You will do well in life."

"Purohit ji, you must have travelled to several places. If you have time, can you please tell me about the various temples that you have visited?" Shankar was particularly interested in the temple that he had seen in his last dream, but he knew that he could not ask it straight forward. It would arouse suspicion.

The priest told him about a few temples in and around the village. But none appeared similar to what he was interested in.

"Purohit ji, we have temples of Shiva, Vishnu and other Gods. Is it true that there are more temples of Gods than Goddesses?" Shankar was trying to give a direction to the conversation.

The priest smiled, "Not at all Shankar, in fact, there would be more temples of Goddesses than Gods. Apparently, while men do not appear to be treating women as their equal, it appears that the balance tilts in favor of Goddesses when it comes to idols. There are several temples of Durga, Laxmi, Saraswati and Chandi for example. There is a ..."

Before the priest could complete his sentence, Shankar asked, "Purohit ji, I am aware of the story of Durga, Laxmi and Saraswati, but I don't know about Chandi so well. Can you please tell me more about her?"

"Not today, Shankar, I have not yet completed my work. Why don't you come tomorrow again? Come a bit earlier. I will tell you the story. Tell your mother that you will have your lunch here with me," said the priest. Shankar left for home, partly confused, partly curious about what may unfold tomorrow.

Chapter 4

A Discovery

"Where are you going so early in the morning?" Shankar's mother asked. She was glad to see Shankar happy. She could feel the glow on his face.

"I am going to the Shiva temple. I have finished my breakfast and Purohit ji said that I can have lunch with him at the temple today. He is going to give me some celestial guidance today," quipped Shankar.

Whatever it was, his mother was happy that Shankar was getting on with his life after the brutal bashing he had over a month back.

"Namaskar, Purohit ji," said Shankar in an excited voice. The temple priest was talking to a small group of people. These people were carrying drums and some other musical instruments with them.

"May God bless you, my child. You have come at the right time," said the priest. "I will take a few minutes with these guests. You go and sit inside please."

The priest joined Shankar after a few minutes. He was very excited that he may get some clue to the last dream that he had seen. After all, the priest had travelled to a lot many places and it was less likely that he would have missed the temple that he had dreamt about.

"These people are Shiva devotees. They keep moving from one village to another and keep singing and enacting folklore about Shiva. They are going to enact the episode of *Sati* today after lunch at the temple," said the priest.

"Now with your query about Chandi, she is the fiercest form of Shakti or Parvati, the wife of Lord Shiva..." the priest continued explaining Shankar the various intricacies about Chandi.

"Shankar, now let us have some food, my son. After that, we can see the act of that folk group. And then if you are not tired, we can continue with our discussion," said the priest.

His wife served them rice, daal and vegetable. During the lunch also, the priest kept telling Shankar various episodes of Chandi. Shankar was attentively listening to the stories.

"Come, now we shall watch the group perform. A lot of devotees are also expected in the temple," said the priest wiping his mouth with the towel after rinsing.

There were a total of six people in the folk group. One had dressed himself like a woman while another had dressed himself like Shiva, also equipped with a fake snake around his neck. He had also managed to fix something resembling a moon crescent over his hair.

One among them started with his damroo, sort of announcing that the act was about to start.

The act was about Sati, who had been born as the daughter of Daksha. While Daksha hated Lord Shiva, Sati, who was an incarnation of Parvati, was deeply in love with him.

"I am organising a sacred offering. Please send invitations to all Gods except that cheat Shiva," exclaimed one person who was acting as the arrogant Daksh.

"I must go Lord Shiva, even though my father has not invited me," said the one who had dressed as Sati.

"I cannot stop you dear, but it is inappropriate to go to a place where you have not been invited," said the one who had dressed like Shiva.

Shankar was attentively watching the whole act.

An angry Daksh had forgotten his love for his daughter. His hatred towards Shiva had overpowered him. "I do not want to keep any relationship with that cheat who wanders in the crematoriums with his gang of cripples. He is no more than a fake to me…" continued the banter.

Unable to bear the humiliation, Sati jumped into the fire immolating herself.

Lord Shiva, when he learned about it, became extremely angry. Unable to control his rage, he plucked a lock of his hair and broke it into two with his leg, creating Virabhadra and Bhadrakali, two fearsome beings.

The person, who had dressed like Shiva, then took a dummy which was then thrown on the ground. The dummy was made to look like a half-burnt Sati. As Shiva wandered around, another person dressed as Lord Vishnu, cut the half-burnt corpse into pieces.

The crowd in the temple was awe struck with the performance. Shankar himself could feel goose bumps on his body. He shifted from one place to another to have a better glimpse of the performance.

"And that my friends, created the Shakti-peeths on earth," said the one who was compering.

Shankar could hardly hear anything. He quickly stepped out of the temple. He wanted the solitude of his house where he could put his thoughts together. His pace was little faster than usual. But his thoughts were running at a much faster pace.

How could he not see the connection? He had been a Shiva disciple since his childhood. He was feeling embarrassed that he couldn't figure out one of the most obvious options.

When Vishnu cut the half-burnt corpse of Sati into pieces, it fell on to various places. Some say that there were fifty-one pieces while others say that there were sixty-four pieces. He had heard about a temple by the side of the holy river, Ganges, in a village in Mithila itself. It was known as Chandi Asthan, in present day Munger. It was quite famous and is said to be very old. Folklore suggests that Karna had paid his obeisance at the temple.

Could it be the one that he had dreamt about? Well, there was only one way to know and Shankar was determined to learn more.

Chapter 5

Visit to Chandi Asthan

"Mother, my destiny is calling me. Please allow me to go. For over a decade, someone has been trying to tell me something. I do not know whether it is good or bad, or if I would be risking my life by exploring my dream. But I know for sure that if my curiosity is not fulfilled, I will not find peace," pleaded Shankar.

His parents did not want to let him go. For one, they knew nothing about Chandi Asthan. Was the dream really trying to tell him something or was it just a mere coincidence? Second, the temple was quite far away and it would take almost full day to reach there by bullock cart. Shankar had just been recovering from the attack last month. Was he strong enough to take the unnecessary physical stress?

"If you are so adamant, then we will also go along with you," said his mother with teary eyes.

But Shankar responded, "No mother, this is my calling. I don't know what lies ahead, but I have to explore it and quench my thirst myself."

His father nodded reluctantly, "Let him go." They both loved their son very much but they also knew that it was really his calling. He had to face whatever lay ahead.

The next morning, his parents bid farewell to Shankar as he climbed on a bullock cart on the way to Chandi Asthan. He had taken the copper plate on which he had engraved the details, some food for the journey and some money.

He was as excited as a cocoon would be on the verge of transforming into a butterfly. It felt as though he was about to meet his long-lost love. The hope of finding long-sought answers thrilled him, but the nervousness of the unknown tied his stomach in knots. He was like a child going to school for the first time - spirited, yet subdued and apprehensive!

The bullock cart stopped at the next village to pick up two more people. They appeared like traders. Shankar bowed to them. "Bless you my child," the elder one said with a warm smile. "Up to where you are going?" he asked.

"I am on my way to Chandi Asthan," said Shankar. He was barely able to hide his child like excitement.

"Good! It's a holy place. That village is blessed. Its glory goes back to the days of Mahabharata and Ramayana. During Ramayana, Sita performed her first Chhath Puja on the banks of Kashtaharni Ghat. Her footprints are still visible on a rock in the river Ganga, and locals have built a temple around it. A few miles away, there is another holy site called Sita Charan, which has a hot water spring named after her—Sita Kund. There are also four ponds named after her four brothers: Rama, Bharat, Laxman, and Shatrughna. Interestingly, only Sita Kund has hot water inside it, rest four ponds have just normal temperature. It is believed that when Sita came back from Lanka, Rama asked her to walk through a pyre of fire to prove her chastity. It is believed that after walking through the fire, Sita took bath in the nearby pond. The pond could not absorb the immense heat from her body and that's why it has always remained hot. The water is said to have divine properties. Several patients have cured themselves of critical diseases by taking a dip in Sita Kund.

"Chandi Asthan itself is one of the famous Shakti-peeths across many kingdoms. Munger was also a part of Anga during the Mahabharata. One of the hills is called Karna Chaura, where it is said that Karna prayed at Chandi Asthan every day. Impressed by his devotion, the deity granted him 114 pounds of gold to distribute among the poor," the elder trader said.

Shankar paused, reflecting on the significance of it all. The stories seemed to weave into his own destiny, pulling him deeper into the mystery he had been seeking.

"But the bullock cart will stop quite a few miles before the temple. The temple is at far end of the village. How do you plan to cover that distance?" the elder trader asked.

"It would also get darker by the time the bullock cart stops," added other trader.

The bullock cart stopped a little while later for a break. The men got down to drink water and the driver of the cart fed grass to the bulls. "Shankar, you can spend the night with me at the sarai. Then, in the morning, you can find some carriage for the temple. I am sure you would find some other devotees too who would be going," the elder trader said. Shankar nodded in agreement. He did not even have any other plan.

When they reached the sarai, the two traders bid good bye to the driver.

"Come Shankar, we will spend the night here. Take some rest. It was a long journey. We will have dinner together," he said.

Shankar washed his feet, hands and face. He lied down on the bed inside the room. Tired heavily, he soon fell asleep only to be woken up by an elderly lady few minutes later.

"Come my child, dinner is ready. If you sleep more now, you will not be able to sleep in the night." Shankar stood up with his eyes barely open. He was slow in getting up. He had thought that the lady would have gone by now. But to his surprise, he saw the lady staring at his arm with her mouth open. Her thin and frail arm rose to touch his birth mark.

"Hmm, I was just checking if this is real," she smiled. She left to fetch food from the kitchen. Shankar kept looking at the old lady. The smile that had adorned her face looking at his birthmark stayed on her face even when she returned with the food. She sat beside Shankar and kept swinging a small fan at him. He felt embarrassed. He asked her to stop but she didn't.

After the dinner, Shankar said, "Amma, I saw a sudden smile on your face when you saw my birthmark. Have you seen it before?"

The old lady signaled him to sit beside her. "You know, you remind me of someone." She almost went into a dream herself. "Many decades ago, I once went to the Chandi Asthan temple along with my parents. There, before the prayer, we had gone to take bath in the Ganges. But I somehow slipped into the river. When I woke up, I found a small group of people near me. The son of the temple priest had saved my life! When I looked at him, I instantly fell in love with him. He was a tall and very muscular man. But you know, he was a Brahman and I was from a different caste. My parents were against it. When they realized that I liked him, they hurriedly married me off. Well, life treated me well after that also, but I never really forgot him. He still occupies a place in my heart! When I saw the mark on your arm, his memories came back in a flash," she concluded, with tears rolling down her cheeks.

Shankar was very excited to hear about this. After all, he knew only about his mother who had shared his birthmark. Now it seems someone completely unconnected also had the same birthmark. Or was there a connection that he was about to discover?

"Is he still there at the temple?" he asked excitedly.

"No, he died off pretty young. He did not marry until later in life. He had gone to some other village. When he returned, he developed a fever which took him away," sighed the old lady.

"Amma, during those days, did you also come across anyone else having the same birthmark?" asked Shankar.

"Not really, in fact, I had asked him about it. He said that it ran in his family. His father and grandfather also had the same," said the old lady.

Shankar suddenly asked, "Amma, do you remember if his father was also very muscular?"

The old lady appeared mused, "Hmm, now that I try to recall, yes. You know, I had seen his father too. Both were too muscular to be a Brahman. But how does that matter?"

In his last dream, Shankar had seen that the light emanating from the crystal over the Shivalinga had made the seven stronger. Was there some kind of magic in the crystal which made them stronger?

***

The next day, he rode another bullock cart which was taking few devotees to Chandi Asthan. The carriage was moving at its own sweet pace but his heart was racing much faster. What if it was not the same temple that he had dreamt about? There were other Shakti-peeths also. Even if it was the same temple, what if he didn't find the Shivalinga? His mind was filled with lots of questions.

The nervous spell inside his head was suddenly broken by chants of "Rama naam satya hai" from a procession nearby. A group of people was returning after saying last prayers to a departed soul. It suddenly filled Shankar with sadness. But his curiosity had grown. He remembered that on both East and West side of the temple, there was one crematorium each. The funeral procession meant that they were near to the temple.

Just a few moments later, he could see smoke coming out from a distance. His fellow travelers bowed in that direction. He found himself following them. His heart was beating faster. Moments later, he could see a triangular mast of the temple. As he got closer, he could see three green leaves over its saffron background. It was exactly the same as he had seen in his dream. He raised his head. The temple compound was large and unwalled. Even from a distance, he could make out several smaller temples within.

"Be careful!" shouted the driver of the carriage as Shankar almost jumped out with his belongings as soon as they reached the temple. Shankar fell on the ground but quickly regained his composure with the help of his stick. He bowed again and entered the temple. He hurried like a kid going to his favorite toy store. Towards his right, he saw a small temple devoted to Lord Shiva and his family. The stone idols of several Gods and Goddesses adorning the temple wall were exactly like what he had seen in his dream.

On the left, there was a statue of Lord Hanuman. There was a walkway directing the devotees to the sanctum sanctorum. He bowed again touching the ground with his hand. There were only a few people ahead of him. Waiting eagerly for his turn, he could see ahead of himself that the walkway was leading him into a dark place. Smoke and pious smell of incense sticks was coming out from the sanctum sanctorum. Ringing the bell above his head, he realized the walkway led devotees into a cave.

He entered inside the poorly lit area, with folded hands. He saw that on the wall of the cave, a large eye had been made. On the side, there was a small Shivalinga and idols of Ganesha and Kartikeya. He felt goosebumps on his arms. As his arm touched a burning incense stick, he finally felt as if the distance between the two worlds - reality and his dreams, had been bridged! Tears started flowing from his eyes. There was not much space inside but he kept standing for a while and prayed to the Goddess, "Please show me the way ahead!"

❁ ❁ ❁

Chapter 6
An Abrupt End?

He spoke with the temple priest, a small, pot-bellied man, and took shelter under him. The priest had taken pity on him. Shankar said that he would sweep the floor and help in other duties at the temple in exchange for the food and shelter.

The local folklore said that when Lord Vishnu cut the half-burnt corpse of Sati, the part of her body that fell at this place was her eye. He quietly took out the copper plate in the night and engraved an eye above the temple.

Shankar stayed there for a few days, talking with people and trying to get some clues. But nobody alluded to a Shivalinga that he was looking for. He even visited few of the nearby smaller temples. He visited some Shiva temples as well, but none fit the bill.

He became restless. How he wanted the nightmares to return to him even if they were scary, only if they could come with some more guidance, with little more direction!

The temple was on the bank of river Ganga. One night, he just could not sleep. All the frustration that had been building over the past few days had become almost unbearable. As soon as the first rays of morning crept inside his room, he stepped into the Ganga to take his daily bath. He knew little bit of swimming but not much. He felt something moving near his feet. Nervous at what it could be, he tried to get away quickly. But instead of coming to the shore, he moved unknowingly farther away into the river. The water was deep there. It almost reached his back. Already tired due to lack of sleep, he panicked. He started to swim. But the current was too strong. He struggled to get to the shore. Although he was not drowning, he was pushed to the shore few feet away from the temple. He caught hold of a small tree there and quickly came out of the water. He lay down to catch his breath. When he opened his eyes, it appeared as if he had seen that place somewhere. He tried to focus more when he realized that this was the place that he had seen from where the six men and the godly figure emerged from the tunnel in his dream.

Had he finally reached the tunnel that he was searching for? Was he a step closer to the Shivalinga and its magical crystal eye? Was the crystal eye really magical or could his hypothesis be false? All kinds of questions were filling inside his mind.

He found a long branch which he could use as a stick. He then stepped in the water to probe it with the stick. He realized that a little away, when he probed, he was able to insert the stick into what appeared like a cavelike structure fully drowned under water.

As he stepped closer to have a better look, he slipped. The fast current quickly overpowered him and he slipped farther away into the river. He was already tired and had little knowledge of swimming. Moments later, he drowned.

Shankar's sufferings, years of nightmares, and his quest also drowned into the mighty Ganges. What was left behind were only few unsolved questions – did the cave really hide the Shivalinga that Shankar had dreamt of? Was there any connection at all between the crystal eye on the Shivalinga and the birthmark on his shoulder?

Well, the copper plate left behind by Shankar did hold a clue to which someone else would latch on to, but centuries later…

Chapter 7
Attila, The Hun

In the fifth century AD, the Huns from Central Asia were terrorizing Europe and Asia. These tribal were ruthless marauders only aiming at destruction and loot. They had already killed the Persian prince and terrorized Constantinople. After establishing their foothold in Gandhar, they turned their evil eyes towards the rich Indian subcontinent. At that time, Northern India was ruled by Skandagupta, a scion of the mighty Gupta Empire. Although they were defeated by Skandagupta, they had managed to make some inroads in the North Western India. Few had even stayed back, married with locals and made India their home. But their instincts remained the same. They were often involved in criminal activities. Few organized gangs and indulged in robbery.

One such Hun, Attila, had been involved in several temple robberies. Attila was the son of a commander in the Hun army. His father had been killed by one of his own soldiers. Attila was only fourteen years old at that time. Upon learning this, he freed the soldier who had killed his father from prison, severed his head apart and hung it from the tree opposite his house. As the news reached his father's seniors in the army, they recruited Attila in the army. Attila had a big muscular built. Feed a person arson, savagery and death in such a tender age and you get another of the same cult. In one of the battles, the enemy had sliced him across his forehead. While Attila immediately killed the enemy, the scar stayed with him forever.

Although the Huns were repulsed by Skandagupta, some of the Huns could not go back either because they were caught or because they hid in the jungles fearing that their tired body and mind would not be able to survive the long and tortuous march back home. Attila also hid in the jungle with few of his men. Several of them died due to diseases and animal attacks in the jungle. As they reached a river, Attila managed to find a boat. He reached a village and soon mingled with the locals. Having been in India for a long time, he spoke the language fluently. He settled there and gradually recovered his health. But with his physical strength, his darker desires also returned. He robbed the temple and ran away with the loot one night. Soon, this became his occupation. He would settle for few days in a village and rob the local temple. He would use his boat to move along the Ganga to avoid getting caught.

Slowly, he reached Pataliputra and then subsequently, Munger. Attila knew from the beginning that the primary reasons for the Huns invading India was to loot the immense wealth lying in the Indian temples. Hence, while he had left his roots behind, he could not leave the greed that had penetrated him so deeply.

His modus operandi was simple. He would find the oldest temple in a particular region. His thought was simple that the older the temple, the higher the number of offerings it would have witnessed over time. Upon reaching Munger, he similarly zeroed in on Chandi Asthan. He was sure that he would find a good haul of treasure there.

***

He first visited Chandi Asthan in the day time. He bowed in front of the deity and spent some time surveying the temple and its surroundings. He spent a few days understanding the temple's history, its priests, the surroundings and the traffic at various hours of the day. He saw that the temple was on the banks of Ganga and it would be quite easy to escape from there. There were only two rooms at the boundary of the courtyard. He learned that one was a store room while the other was where the priest and his family lived. Just at the entry of the sanctum sanctorum, there was a big and strong box for collecting donation from the devotees. It had a heavy lock on it. The donation box made him smile. The heavier and stronger the box, the more the collections, he knew it well by now. After a few days, during the evening, he saw the priest directing few strong men to take the filled donation box towards the store room. Now he knew what he had to do.

That very night, he quietly broke into the store room. He was astonished to see several donation boxes kept there. They had big locks guarding them. But no lock was big enough for the skills that Attila had. It appeared as if the locks had not been opened for ages. Most were covered with layers of dust. He took out a small tool box. It had a bunch of wires of varying lengths and thicknesses. He wasn't interested in just any box. His hypothesis was that the people of ancient ages were more liberal with their donations and hence, the chance of finding offerings of higher value was much higher in the older boxes. He looked around and zeroed in on what appeared to be the oldest box to him. There was another box on it. He removed it quietly. It was pretty heavy; But Attila himself was quite strong, having been a soldier just few years ago. The box that Attila was interested in had rusted on the sides. The lock looked strong, but the handle had not been able to take the toll of years and years of rust.

As soon as Attila held the lock, the handle broke on its own. He tried to open the box. But due to the rust, the box made a creaking sound while opening. Attila carefully opened the box. It was night and even the slightest sound would be sufficient to wake up the priest next door.

As soon as he opened the box, Attila was bedazzled to see the contents inside it. There were several large pearls, a big gold necklace, precious gems so big that he had never seen before and a copper plate in which something seemed to have been engraved. He took out his bag and started filling it with whatever he could get his hands on. He knew that he could not take it all with him, not even all contents of the first box that he had opened. He tied his bundle of loot and carried the copper plate under his arm.

He swiftly moved out of the store room without raising any alarm. He had tied his boat on the shore. He quickly rowed it away from the temple.

He rowed furiously, putting as much distance as possible between himself and the shore. Though pleased with his plunder, his gaze kept returning to the copper plate. Under the moonlight, he examined it closely, his breath catching at the sight of the crystal eye embedded in the Shivalinga.

"People donate lots of things to the temples. I have seen all kinds of valuables. Some even donate a part of their labor so that the blessings make them flourish in their profession. But a copper plate like this?" thought Attila.

The contours engraved on the plate resembled Chandi Asthan. Even the deity was the same. So definitely it was something related to the Chandi Asthan that he had robbed a little while back. But then there was no Shivalinga in the temple like that shown on the plate!

He looked at the plate. The Shivalinga encapsulated the wheel, its seven spokes and the eyes made on each spoke. The rays shown emanating from the crystal eye above the wheel looked like a halo he had seen on the heads of Gods and Goddesses. Was it a part of the temple that existed in ancient times? Could it be that the Shivalinga was either destroyed or robbed? Or was it situated somewhere near Chandi Asthan? The Shivalinga was engraved outside the boundary of the temple shown on the plate. He said to himself, "This is more likely."

Perhaps he could rob Chandi Asthan again instead of looking for this new temple. But he had never robbed the same temple twice in order to avoid suspicion. And he did not want to make any exception here either.

But how could he know more about it? He had carefully studied the area around Chandi Asthan. He had neither seen anything like that nor come across any mention of it. But the image on the plate suggested that the Shivalinga had to be nearby only. Where could he learn more about such an ancient statue?

❁ ❁ ❁

Chapter 8
Attila Reaches Nalanda

Attila knew that just like the Huns, several Chinese travelers had been to this part of India, although not in pursuit of wealth but wisdom. Unlike most ancient Indian knowledge which remained largely verbal, the Chinese believed in scripting their experiences. There was a high chance that if such a Shivalinga existed, someone or the other could have written about it. In last few years, Attila had gathered quite a huge amount of wealth robbing temples in India. But more than the wealth, he somehow had become addicted to the act itself- the trick of finding old temples, zeroing in where the wealth could be located and looting it without being caught. The copper plate or rather the mysterious Shivalinga and its crystal eye, now became a mission for Attila.

He knew that several learned men from India and other countries used to study at the famous university of Nalanda. Many of the Chinese travelers had also landed there upon visiting India. "That is where I need to go next," he thought.

Nalanda's history dates back to 1,200 BCE. In the third century BCE, the great emperor Ashoka had built a temple there. Gautam Buddha is said to have delivered lectures at Nalanda. There were several monasteries built, where people from as far as Tibet, China, Indonesia, Turkey, Japan, Korea and Persia used to come, stay and study various subjects along with other Indian scholars.

Attila took three days to reach Nalanda. He enquired to learn that the university had a library called Dharmaganja. It had three large multistoried buildings. He was awe-struck by the buildings.

A passerby looked at Attila. "What you see is Dharmaganja, the largest library of the world. There are three buildings- Ratnasagar (ocean of jewels), Ratnaranjaka (jewel adorned) and Ratnodadhi (sea of jewels). All are nine storied buildings. As you can see, all the main pillars have numerous small carvings of sitting Buddha on their circumference. The walls are adorned with Buddha in various postures. The architecture is such that it allows ample amount of sunshine to light the rooms inside during the day. There are large windows which allow ample ventilation in order to keep the air fresh inside. Thousands of manuscripts are kept inside. These cover subjects like religion, literature, astronomy, medicine, philosophy and others. There are so many scholars who come here from across the world in order to study. They also stay here and translate various scriptures into foreign languages and vice versa. There is a lot of knowledge exchange that happens behind these walls. It is no less than a temple." He carried on without waiting for a response from Attila.

While the access to the scriptures was restricted, the entry to the buildings was not. "There could be thousands and thousands of scriptures here. How am I going to find what I am looking for?" thought Attila.

He mingled with few of the junior scholars and tried to understand more about the university and the wealth of knowledge that was lying there. The more he interacted, the more convinced he was that finding relevant information about the Shivalinga drawn on the copper plate would be like finding a needle in a stack of hay.

What now?" The thought echoed in his mind. A senior faculty member… perhaps. But who? Who could he… use? The scriptures. He needed the scriptures. The idea took root, cold and calculating. His enquiries revealed that one of the most senior scholars was Aryabhat. He was a reputed astronomer and had scripted several studies which were revered by other scholars. Attila also learnt that Aryabhat had made a sun dial at one of the Sun temples at a nearby village. It appeared to Attila that Aryabhat was not only an astronomer but also an ardently religious man. "Maybe I can take his help. But why would he help me? If he knows that I am only looking for treasure, he would not help me for sure. Can there be some weakness that I can exploit?" Attila thought.

He continued to enquire about Aryabhat from different people. He was being cautious so that no one suspected him. He would talk to two or three persons only, that too at different places of the village. Aryabhat had written a book called *Aryabhatiya.* The book had claimed quite a reputation among the scholars. It appeared that he was also writing another one Arya-siddhanta. The latter was supposed to be closer to his heart and mostly on astronomical computations.

One day, after completing his evening prayer, Aryabhat was returning to his room at the university. "Who's there?" Aryabhat was surprised to find someone sitting inside his room on the chair. A small lamp sat on the table nearby. The dark silhouette suggested a large muscular built and the dimly lit room made it look scary. Aryabhat was almost sixty years old. He didn't have much of a treasure that anyone could be interested in. He was a noble man and had not harmed anyone. So he was not scared, but puzzled nonetheless. Moreover, Nalanda was a peaceful village and the university was a seat of learning with no criminal activity inside. "What do you want?"

The stranger slowly increased the glow of the lamp until there was ample light inside the room. "Sir, I am just a curious traveler. I trade in antique treasures. I…," said Attila. But before he could complete what he was saying, Aryabhat said in a stern voice, "I am a scholar. If you are looking for knowledge, there is a wealth of treasure I have. But the worldly ones, I possess none. Please leave from here. I am tired from a hectic day and I want to rest now."

"Aryabhat, you don't know me. But you could still help me. I am looking for some information. I strongly believe it could be there in the scriptures inside the Dharmaganja. But I do not know how to read. More so, there are so many scriptures. I do not know where to look for. I want you to look for it in there," said Attila. The salutation was more direct, the tone had changed this time and Aryabhat did not miss out on these.

"But if you do not know how to read and write, how will you be sure that I will tell you the truth? I might just say that the information you are looking for, just doesn't exist or I might just mislead you to get you off my back. How will you know?" said Aryabhat.

Attila was not a scholar. He didn't know to read or write. But travails of a rough life are no less. They teach you numerous means of survival that no book could ever tell you about.

"Perhaps this could keep you under check," said Attila.

"Give that back to me," shouted a frail Aryabhat looking at what Attila had in his hand. It was not difficult to identify the work that he had been trying to complete since last so many years- Arya-siddhanta. It was not only his work but the only true love he ever had. Aryabhat had been studying planetary systems since long and had formulated several fundamentals which had not been proved by anyone so far. He had collected numerous data over decades to prove his numerous findings. A loss of the book could push the world back by several centuries till someone else found those scientific principles.

"Sit down, Aryabhat. I mean no harm. This book means nothing to me. But it does contain the studies that you have done for God knows how many decades. Honestly, I am a very focused man. Give me what I want and I will give this book to you. Till that time, the book stays safe with me," said Attila with a faint smile on his face.

"But why should I believe you? Suppose I find it. How can I be sure that you will hand over the book to me? It means nothing to you. And what if the information that you are seeking doesn't even exist? How will you believe me then?" asked a worried Aryabhat. Beads of perspiration could be seen on his cheek.

"Well, I am an honest man, Aryabhat. As I said, there is nothing of importance for me in this book. If I am convinced that there is no such information, or as soon as you help me with that, I promise that I will give it back to you," said Attila. He then opened his bag and said, "Look at this copper plate. There is a Shivalinga crafted on it. It seems to have a unique crystal eye made on it. I am looking for information on this one. This must be housed in some ancient temple. I have come across several such ancient temples, which lost their glory with time but were very famous places of worship during their age. I am sure that someone or the other would have come across it and written something about it which may help me find it. I need your help in finding the same". He was very calm in his composure while Aryabhat was almost fuming at the stupidity of the bargain- his whole life worth of findings versus some ancient temple which may or may not exist.

But Aryabhat was mature enough to understand that the odds were against him. Whatever the case may be, he just had to give an honest try. Attila may or may not heed to his promise, but there was no option left for him. He took a good look at the copper plate. The details of the Shivalinga got etched in his mind- the numerous small snakes surrounding it, the wheel with seven spokes and the sparkling eye above it.

Chapter 9
Aryabhat Gets to Work

The very next morning, he took Attila along to Dharmaganj. "How do we know in which era did that particular Shivalinga existed?" asked Aryabhat. His mind was working at a rapid pace. After all, a life full of his learning was at stake. Without waiting for an answer, he said, "Although there are several old scriptures here, a description like this is more likely to be found in one of the travelogues. But the earliest ones here are just a century old." He quickly paced along with Attila to one of the rooms. The room had a nice smell. Aryabhat remarked that the library burned certain incense sticks which repelled bookworms and kept freshness around.

After few hours of search, they didn't find anything remotely connected with the Shivalinga. Without breaking for lunch, they continued. "Let us go to another part of the library," said Aryabhat. This room looked even older. Although scriptures looked worn out with time, the room itself was kept neat and tidy. Attila was amazed to see that there was sufficient lighting inside. There was no cobweb and there was a strange freshness in the air.

He moved to one of the shelves. "Don't touch anything, my dear friend," Aryabhat said in a stern voice. "These are very precious and fragile too."

Attila sat on a small chair kept there. He helped Aryabhat in positioning the ladder for picking books from the upper shelves whenever Aryabhat wanted. Aside from a few monosyllables, silence reigned until evening. By then, they had searched three rooms without finding anything related to the Shivalinga.""Let's end here today," said Attila. His frustration over lack of any discovery was far more tiring than the physical efforts of Aryabhat.

***

The next evening, they had completed searching the second multistoried building also but in vain. Aryabhat had a lot of patience. After all, he had been studying planetary system for decades and moments of revelation were few. But Attila had no patience. His earlier profession of war and his current occupation of temple robbery- both required less of patience and more of swift action.

"Aryabhat, is this the last section to search?" he asked as they entered the last building of Dharmaganja the fifth day. Aryabhat was also tired, both more mentally than physically. The Arya-siddhanta was a life-time of finding for him and was absolutely of no value to Attila. If he still didn't find anything, would Attila return his book? He was not sure.

"I am trying my best," said a worn out Aryabhat. "There is only one section here that houses older scriptures. Wait for me here."

He spoke with one of the guards there and returned to Attila, "We will have to wait for some time till the chief caretaker comes. He has the keys to the last room left now.

After a long impatient wait, a very muscular man came from the door and looked at both. Seeing that it was Aryabhat, the most renowned person at the university, he bowed respectfully. “Guru ji, what brings you here?”

“I need the key to the Garbha. I also need to take this person inside. He is with me. He has come from a long way and needs to check on some information,” said Aryabhat to the caretaker.

“But Guru ji, you know that no one is allowed there. Why don’t you go alone and let him sit here till the time you return?” said the caretaker with his head still bowed.

Aryabhat was already frustrated. “Do as I say. Just open the door. We are in a hurry and will not take much time.”

Attila was standing beside Aryabhat just listening to the conversation without opening his mouth. He knew that he could not force himself there. The caretaker himself was stronger than him. Plus he could call other guards and they would nab him in no time. He was just amazed that there was no door inside the room where they were standing. Which room were they talking about? Was it some kind of signal to get him caught?

The caretaker was surprised with Aryabhat’s demeanor. He said, “If you insist Guru ji. I would request you to please stand outside while I open the door.”

As soon as Aryabhat and Attila came out of the room, the caretaker closed the door. Attila was alarmed. Could this be a trap? Behind the door, he could hear loud clinkering voices at times. After some time, the caretaker opened the door and let them in. Attila was awestruck to see that where he was unable to find any door a little while back, was almost twenty feet by forty feet door open ajar.

"We will be back in sometime," said Aryabhat as they entered the hidden room opened up by the caretaker. As soon as they entered, the door closed on its own. It was suddenly dark everywhere. Attila was sweating now fearing that he was finally caught. Was it the end of his dream? Trying to terrorize the most renowned scholar and more importantly, trying to search an ancient holy crystal from the purpose of stealing it could attract severe punishment. He was still thinking his options when he heard a knob turning nearby.

"This part of Dharmaganja houses the oldest secrets known to us. They are very fragile and susceptible to damage. There is a complex web of mirrors which gets actuated once the knob is turned. This brings in the sunlight inside the room," said Aryabhat the next moment. Attila forced a smile on his face, wiping the sweat off his forehead.

There were several antique scriptures there. There was a big writing on the wall in front of them. "What is written there," asked Attila.

Aryabhat replied, "It is an instruction for handling of scriptures here. It says- save me from water, protect me from oil, and from loose binding, and do not give me into the hands of fools."A wry smile came on his face.

Attila saw that most of the writings were on papyrus. Some were in the shapes of rolls, few others in form of flip books with strong binding at the edge. Aryabhat opened a few of them. But he could not find anything. He frantically searched here and there but his face had started showing the frustration. "Look, we have searched this one as well. Unfortunately, I don't see anything even remotely related to your Shivalinga," said a disappointed Aryabhat.

He then actuated some lever which opened the door which they had come from. "We are done. Thank you for your kind help," Aryabhat said to the caretaker. As they were going, Attila turned around, but he could not see the door from which they emerged only a while back. Where did it vanish? But he had more important things to worry about as they had not found anything about the Shivalinga.

Both Attila and Aryabhat walked away quietly. As soon as they came out of Dharmaganja, Aryabhat asked, "Where did you find this copper plate?" He himself was not one to give up easily, more so, when his Arya-siddhanta was at stake.

"There is a temple on the bank of river Ganga-Chandi Ashthan Asthan, in a city called Munger. I found it there," said Attila, lost in his thoughts.

"What a fool you are! You have wasted so much of my time. If you found it there, should you not search there?" shouted an angry Aryabhat.

"Well, I had done a good recce of the area before robbing the temple. I didn't find or hear anything resembling it. So I thought that even if it was located physically there somewhere, it was not in the living memory of the inhabitants. How could one find it if no one living actually knew anything about it? There are no clues on the copper plate. That's when I thought that maybe I could try looking for any reference to it in the older scriptures here," said Attila in a defensive tone.

❊ ❊ ❊

Chapter 10
Back to Chandi Asthan

Inquisitiveness is a basic nature of scientists. And Aryabhat was never at peace with an unsolved riddle at hand, even if it was not related to his immediate line of work. After all, he had successfully extrapolated several such unrelated experiences in the past to find solutions for his quests.

"Look, I can give one more try. We must first look at the place where you found this thing. That would be the easiest thing to do," said Aryabhat with a command that didn't ask for Attila's permission. Attila just nodded.

The only thing was that Attila was little worried that it was only few days back that he had looted the temple. What if he was caught? But the last time, he had used a fake beard and moustache to hide his identity. It would be really difficult for anyone to find him out. But wouldn't two strangers asking questions about the copper plate raise fresh suspicion?

He raised his concern to Aryabhat. To his satisfaction, Aryabhat replied that they would not make any enquiry from the people. Attila was also confident that the presence of a renowned person like Aryabhat would not raise any suspicion.

At Chandi Asthan, although people had not forgotten about the robbery, there was nothing much one could do. Things were normal once again with a new lock at the store-room. When Aryabhat and Attila reached the temple, they bowed to the deity. When the priest came, Aryabhat spoke to him, "Pandit ji, my name is Aryabhat. I am…"

Even before he could complete, the priest started, "Aryabhat from Nalanda?" Aryabhat nodded in affirmative. How blessed we are to have you here! Please let us know how we can assist you," said the priest. Then, turning to Attila, he asked, "And you? Have we met before?" His expression betrayed a hint of confusion.

Aryabhat was also not sure what to say. And he wanted to divert priest's attention. He hurriedly said, "I hear that this place has had earthquakes in the past. We are doing some studies regarding the same. We want to stay for a few days so that we can carry out our study." Attila took advantage of the discussion between Aryabhat and the priest and stealthily moved back away from the priest.

The priest answered, "Sure. My attendant will show you a house. It's completely furnished and we use it for housing guests. It even has a fully equipped kitchen. But if you need anything else, please let me know."They retired for the rest of the day tired fully from the journey they had had in reaching the temple.

***

The next day, unsure of what Aryabhat was up to, Attila asked, "What is your plan now?"

Aryabhat said, "First, let us try to know more about this village, its people and its history. Then we might get some clue. If we don't, then we need to carry out our own exploration. I am still not sure if we will find anything. But since you have involved me now, I want to give it a try. This is the last option I can think of. After that, whether you return my Arya-siddhanta or not, I have nothing to do with you."

Attila appeared on a back foot. He knew that Aryabhat had given a good try. He was also not sure if they would find anything, but he didn't have any better plan. He fumbled in a low voice which sounded bereft of any trace of confidence, "I promise to return your book."

"Aryabhat found the priest inside the temple, Pandit ji. My equipment will arrive in a few days. Till that time, please let me know more about the history of this place. I am excited to know more about it."

Pandit ji explained in detail how Munger had a history running back to the days of the greatest epic Mahabharata and even back to Ramayana. Sita had performed her first *chhath puja* on the bank of Kashtaharni Ghat, some distance away from Chandi Asthan. There was another temple, Sita Kund, where Sita was supposed to have given the test of her chastity upon returning from Lanka. Karna was said to have visited Chandi Asthan temple during Mahabharata.

But the stories were not giving much of a clue to Aryabhat. Even Attila was having second thoughts about the Shivalinga-should he not focus on other temples instead of wasting his time on this one? There didn't seem much of a clue. He decided that he would give Aryabhat only a few days. Even if he didn't find it, he would return the Arya-siddhanta to him. After all, Aryabhat commanded a lot of respect in the kingdom. Why invite the ire of the king unnecessarily? There were so many temples that could serve his purpose.

Aryabhat said, "Attila, many ancient places get buried inside earth with time. Archaeologists then carry out excavation to unearth those hidden underneath what is seen from the naked eye. We can carry out some studies to see if any ancient place existed underneath this area. You found the copper plate in Chandi Asthan. So it is likely that the Shivalinga is hidden somewhere nearby. At least, that is the last option left now. Else, it might be anywhere on earth or even a figment of someone's imagination."

With his message, a couple of aides with a few equipment arrived in next three days from Nalanda. Next couple of days, they chose an empty land nearby and flattened it. They created a strong structure about twenty feet high. It had a pulley with which they could pull a large boulder to that height. At a few more places nearby, Aryabhat ordered his men to flatten the earth. Over a wide area, he kept few dome like structures over the flat earth. These domes were kept at sufficient distance from each other. At the top of each dome, a probelike structure was fixed, the tip of which ended against a paper. The paper was tied to a rolling drum.

"We will send sound waves inside the earth. Our domes would act like our ears, catching the sound waves which are reflected from underneath the rocks. The probes would translate the sound waves to vibrations. The drums would be rolling at same speed so that the tip of the probe against the paper would translate the sound waves into a graph. We will have several of these graphs from various domes. If the earth below is a continuous structure everywhere, then we would get the same graphs on all the papers. A significant difference would confirm that the earth is not the same underneath. This may not necessarily mean that the Shivalinga is there. We would then need to excavate further to check," said Aryabhat to Attila.

But Attila was getting more nervous day by day. One, the involvement of several other men had thrown away the physical supremacy he enjoyed over old and frail Aryabhat. Would it be difficult to overpower him and seize the Arya-siddhanta without going ahead with any of these studies? Second, the probability of finding the Shivalinga was looking lower each day. Was it even worth it?

The next day, a big boulder was moved up with chain and pulley up to the structure built twenty feet high. There were few onlookers. They had been asked to stay at a distance so that they didn't get hurt by any untoward instance. Near each dome, there was a weight coming down a pulley. Each weight ensured that each drum to which paper was attached rolled out at the same rotational speed. Each probe against the paper was making a circle of same diameter.

Next moment, Aryabhat shouted, "Drop the boulder!" With a loud thud, the boulder weighing more than five men combined came down with a force that shook the ground below. The depression on the ground was such that the boulder remained in place.

The probes over the domes were making their prints on the papers rotating against them. Attila was standing near one of the domes. He could see that the earlier circular motion of the probe had now broken into small vibrations which were getting recorded on the paper. He was stunned with all these. After a while, the drums stopped rotating. Aryabhat had made a large map and marked their relative position on it. Each paper had been assigned a number and the numbers had been marked on the map. He collected all the papers carefully himself after a while.

During the night, he spread the papers over a board in the hut where he was staying with Attila. He also had the map in front of him. In his book, he kept noting some data. Attila didn't know to read or write. He was just watching Aryabhat work around his way.

Aryabhat then kept working in his note book which appeared more of a series scribbling to Attila. Unable to understand anything, Attila went to sleep. But Aryabhat kept on working on his observations throughout the night. When Attila woke up the next day, Aryabhat was sleeping with several papers strewn here and there. He didn't feel like waking Aryabhat up. He went out to take his bath. When he returned, he found Aryabhat awake.

"So any conclusions you have made?" asked Attila, not very confident of whatever was going on.

Aryabhat opened his note book and showed a rough drawing that he had made. "Sound is reflected differently by materials of different density. Using the data that our study gave us, I have drawn a rough schematic of the ground underneath. In these surrounding areas, you can see that the earth is pretty uniform. But a little away, the light shade represents a hollow tunnel like structure. The blue portion represents the Ganges. So, it appears that the tunnel starts near the bank of the Ganges and goes somewhere far away.

It doesn't end in the region we have mapped. So, there is definitely something one may excavate and explore. But will it lead to your Shivalinga or not, no one can say even now."

Attila was confused. He had already spent quite many days on the Shivalinga. The probability of finding it was increasing, but still very low. He was also missing his family back home. He didn't say anything. During the night, he saw that Aryabhat was making some more marks on the map relative to where they were staying. He didn't show any interest in what Aryabhat was doing.

The next morning, Attila carefully unfolded the map. Aryabhat had been working late, so he was still sleeping. Attila was only interested in the place where the tunnel would be opening near the Ganges. Rest he could discover on his own. He carefully assimilated all that he needed. He carefully wrapped Arya-siddhanta in a leather cover and tied it on his stomach. He didn't need the copper plate anymore.

He folded the map back so as not to arouse any suspicion. He quietly stepped out of the house. He stepped to the Ganges near the temple and tried to locate the tunnel. It appeared that it was some distance away. The bank of the Ganges was dirty and muddy. If he walked on it, he could injure himself. Moreover, if anyone spotted him, it would arouse suspicion. So, he thought of swimming to the tunnel. He stepped inside the Ganges and started swimming. In around ten minutes, he reached what the map had shown as the mouth of the tunnel. He came out of water and started looking nearby. He could not find anything. There were all kinds of wild plants which had taken hold of the area. He found a large stick with which he probed nearby. But he still could not find anything. He was frustrated. Hot sun had started to rise and he was sweating also. He stepped into the water again to see if there was anything on the bank but he could not find anything. Suddenly, he felt something biting on his left foot. He shrieked in pain. When he lifted it, he found a small bite on his foot. It had turned red. The water was muddy, so he could not see anything. He tried coming out of the water, but he felt as if all his energy had been sucked up. Whatever had bitten him, the poison seemed deadly. He tried to take the support of the stick he had but he soon fell into the water.

❁ ❁ ❁

Chapter 11
The End of an Era

When sunlight started coming through the crevices and almost lit the whole room, Aryabhat woke up. He realized that it was almost noon. He woke up reluctantly, tired from the plan he had been making the whole night. Now it would not take much time and he would soon be back at Nalanda along with the work of his life, Arya-siddhanta.

He quickly freshened up and prepared for further studies he wanted to carry out that day. Now that he was sure that there indeed was a tunnel-like structure, he had decided that he would do a seismic mapping of that part. Who knows what all might come up? Maybe he could find the Shivalinga also! He was excited to share his plans with Attila.

Suddenly, Aryabhat realised that he had not seen Attila since the time he had woken up. In fact, even if Aryabhat slept till late, Attila used to get up early and Aryabhat would keep hearing some sound or the other. But he had slept in complete silence that morning. Where was Attila? Aryabhat looked around. He could see the copper plate kept at its usual place. So at least, Attila was still nearby somewhere.

He called his team and moved onto another area in order to set up the seismic studies again. By late evening, the tall structure for throwing the boulder, several domes for listening and converting sound waves into graphs, had been all set up. Aryabhat was still busy directing everyone for the set up. But as soon as the set up was complete, he again started to think about Attila. He had not seen him even once.

Aryabhat became concerned. His Arya-sidhhanta was with Attila. Aryabhat had waited patiently for so long thinking that Attila would return it. It was of no use to Attila anyway. Aryabhat went to the temple and enquired about Attila. No one had seen him. Frustrated, he came to the house where he was staying. He was not able to focus on anything. The copper plate was still there. He took out the copper plate and looked at it. Had Attila left? He had not found the Shivalinga so far. Had he changed his mind?

Suddenly, Aryabhat thought about his map. Could Attila have read the dimensions on the map and left alone to search? But he wasn't literate. Or did he fool him? After all, he was in the army. So there was a high chance that he knew of basic reading and writing in order to communicate with his rank and file. Aryabhat was convinced now that Attila had left. It was late night. Aryabhat was not able to sleep. He rummaged through the belongings of Attila. But he could not find his Arya-siddhanta. Tired both mentally and physically, he fell to sleep on his bed.

There on the bank of the Ganges, the poison was strong enough to put Attila to sleep forever. Strong currents then washed him deeper into the river. His body was never found. And with him washed away years of Aryabhat's findings – Arya-siddhanta.

Back at Chandi Asthan, Aryabhat almost went berserk with loss of his Arya-siddhanta. Years of hard work and findings had gone waste. He cursed the Shivalinga on the copper plate. He felt like finding it and destroying it. He shut all doors and windows and bolted the house from inside. He didn't open the door the next day when his staff came for continuing the studies. They had come with the temple priest.

"Maybe he slept late. Let us try to wake him up after some time," said the priest.

But someone from the group said, "Pandit ji, no matter how late he sleeps, he wakes up early in the morning. In fact, even if he doesn't sleep, he sleeps only the next night, not even during the next day."

Another said, "Unless, he has been disappointed by something, in which case, he shuts himself for days altogether without food and water." They knew Aryabhat well from years of association at the university. They kept coming every morning to check.

On the sixth day, when they came again, they found the door open. A frail looking old man that Aryabhat had turned into in the past few days without food and water, he was sitting outside the house warming himself after his bath. He was eating some fruits. Not the one to answer others, as soon as he saw his men, Aryabhat said, "Let us finish our studies. We have a lot of work to do." The best thing about being a scientist is presence of a lot of hope and optimism. No matter how big a set-back you face, you always find the strength to resurrect and follow your pursuits. Once he was done with exploring this Shivalinga, he could again focus on re-writing Arya-siddhanta.

He shifted his seismic studies to a different place this time in order to get a better understanding. The third time, the data showed the presence of a cylinder like structure, almost six feet in height. Aryabhat was confident that it was the same statue that Attila had been looking for.

The next few days, he studied the position of the sun, its shadows and the position of stars and engraved a set of numbers on the copper plate- 26.5110°N, 84.6884°E.

But his health started faltering. He had to take the help of a wooden stick in order to walk longer distances. "This is definitely an ancient Shivalinga and it would open us to a whole new knowledge about our past. But first I must get better in order to continue my research," thought Aryabhat.

The next day, he briefed his men that he wanted to stop the survey for a few days. He returned to Nalanda with his men. He was not sure where had Attila gone. One part of his brain said that he was gone forever. But what if he returned for the ancient Shivalinga? And why would a robber be after an ancient Shivalinga? Or was there some treasure hiding alongside? It was possible since most ancient temples have been found to be very rich with offerings from devotees over ages.

"Whatever it may be, I will not allow him or anyone else to lay hands on the copper-plate now. I will hide it till I complete my studies and then hand it over to the king for safety once the king comes back from pilgrimage in two months."

For next few days, his health remained the same, in fact, it was declining slowly. He arranged for a large metal pot. The pot was such that it could almost hide a kid of 5-6 years. He prepared a chemical and coated the whole pot with a thick layer of the same. He was doing all this alone and did not allow anyone to see what he was up to.

After few days of hard work, the pot now had a strange look. A thick coat adorned it all over. A vertical line of some other material divided the pot in two symmetrical parts. The line started at the neck of the pot from one side, went through the bottom and then it ended at the neck on the other side. The neck of eighteen inches' diameter had a specially designed mounting over it. At the top, it was closed with a glass.

Aryabhat then asked the caretaker of Garbha at Dharmaganj to move the pot inside. Aryabhat commanded a lot of respect. The caretaker simply complied. Aryabhat then placed the pot in the center of the hidden room, quite away from other books and scriptures kept inside the room. He had written his name on the neck of the pot. That way, no other researcher would dare to open it. He had also attached a small scrap of metal in the front of the pot with few lines scribbled on it.

Aryabhat was happy that he had hidden the copper plate safely inside the pot. He knew that he may not survive for long. What if he could not explore the ancient truth before he died? The metal scrap and the lines written on it held the key to opening the pot. However, he had made it so complex that only a very learned person could open it. Else, it would destroy the content inside.

Aryabhat then took the men who had accompanied him last time to Chandi Asthan. His health was not recovering and he was sad that he was going on a journey that made him lose his Arya-siddhanta. He wanted to go alone. He took one boat while the other men took another. Aryabhat's boat was ahead. He prayed to the rising sun and took a deep breath. He was very near to completing the puzzle. He could then focus on re-writing Arya-siddhanta. Maybe he could include few more principles this time.

His boat moved farther away from that of his men. Soon, his boat went so far that his men could not see him anymore. And that was the last time that anyone had seen Aryabhat. The other men reached Chandi Asthan and went to retire. The next day, they went to the house where Aryabhat was supposed to reside. However, they were surprised to find a lock outside that house. They enquired around but no one had seen Aryabhat or for that matter anyone using that house since last few days. They got worried and started enquiring about Aryabhat in different directions.

Unable to find any answer, they headed back to the place where they had disembarked from the boat. There they heard that a boat expected to come yesterday had not arrived so far and was feared to have capsized. Their heart sank. They prayed for the safety of Nalanda. One of the men headed back to Nalanda to apprise the university and the palace officials of the same. The other men waited for few more days at Chandi Asthan praying and hoping for a miracle. But with each passing day, their hopes also faded away. After almost a week, they headed back to Nalanda.

First, Shankar lost his life - a physically challenged kid with visions of a Shivalinga, gobbled by the mighty Ganges. Then, Attila the Hun – a muscular soldier-turned-robber of a foreign origin lost his life, bitten by something. Along with him, decades of hard work - Arya-siddhanta washed away. Days later, one of the most famous astronomers – Aryabhat drowned in the Ganges.

All died in the pursuit of an antique Shivalinga with a crystal eye that no one even got a chance to look at. Was the Shivalinga cursed? Did it have an evil eye? Did people let it go into oblivion purposefully? Was there really a connection between the eye on Shankar's arm and the one made on the Shivalinga? Or was it a mere coincidence? Only time would tell or perhaps ages!

Chapter 12
The Bhola Cyclone, 1970

Lullabies are normally relaxing for a four-year-old kid. The calm rhythm eases out unfulfilled curiosities and anxieties of the whole day and fills their heart with optimism and hope for tomorrow. But that night was different. Vikram had helped his mother the whole day trying to keep their house intact. At upwards of 185km/hr, the wind was really fierce. He had not seen his father since the morning. He did not even take his normal afternoon nap. He was really tired. He could sense that his mother's voice was quivering. He pretended to appear asleep so that his mother herself stopped singing and took some rest. In between, he would open his eyelids very briefly to watch the tense face of his mother.

He prayed for the return of his father. It was not the first time that his father went out even before he woke up in the morning. From the time he started understanding things, he had seen men leaving their houses early in the morning to hunt for animals or bring fruits for their families. They would return before it was dark outside. After all, darkness could be dangerous inside the jungle in the North Sentinel Island. It was a bit late than usual that day, but he believed that his father would come back soon.

He could sense his mother choking in between the singing. "Mother, are you crying?"

"No dear! Just that there was so much work the whole day that I feel tired now." She said in a low voice.

"Why don't you sleep by my side?"

Vikram's mother quickly lay down beside him. Vikram clinged to her tightly. He remembered that at times when he felt low, his parents would tell him the story of the crystal eye. The story filled him with renewed strength and vigor. He had memorized every single bit of it. In fact, it was the most prevalent folklore on the island. Everyone knew about it. Even his grandfather used to tell the same story before he passed away last year.

Vikram said, "Mother, tonight, let me tell you the story of the crystal eye!"

***

"Long ago, there was a rightful and humble King. There lived a demon in the kingdom disguised as a trader. He was very cunning and used to cheat people. Hearing so many complaints, the King decided to talk to the demon himself.

"He sent his soldiers to bring the demon to his palace. Actually, due to the good work of the King, the palace was blessed by saints and no demon could enter on its own. But an invitation by the King himself was different! It was the chance that the demon had been waiting for since years.

"When the soldiers came, the demon gave a cunning smile and happily came along.

"The King started raising concerns that his people had been telling him about. The demon kept smiling arrogantly. When the King finished his words and asked the demon to clarify his position, the demon started laughing.

"Ha ha ha! These are all true your majesty! I humbly own all my mistakes. But are you strong enough to punish me?

"Having said this, the demon came out of the disguise. He was gigantic in size. His head touched almost the ceiling of the court. He had a big belly. He appeared as if he had not taken bath since ages.

"The whole court was scared. People ran to save their life. The King was speechless. He ordered his soldiers to capture the demon. Few of the soldiers attacked the demon with their bows. But the demon was far too strong for these and the soldiers started to run away.

"The prince was still a twelve-year-old boy. He came to the rescue of the King. But the demon struck the King with his sword. The King was hurt brutally. He was covered in blood all over. The prince quickly pulled the King to his side.

"The dying King told the prince to run away from the kingdom and find the crystal eye.

"One of the ministers pulled the prince away and they escaped to the river through a hidden route. The prince met an old saint who guided him whatever little he knew about the crystal eye. The prince then went in search of the crystal eye.

"After almost a year of searching in difficult terrains, he finally found the crystal eye. It had immense powers. He prayed to the crystal eye. Suddenly, while in deep meditation, he felt rays emanating from the crystal eye into his body.

There was a sudden bright flash and then it was normal again. He became very strong.

"Then he returned to his kingdom. He was sad to see that the demon and his people had taken over the kingdom. He had enslaved the inhabitants, chained them and subjected them to cruelty.

"The prince challenged the demon. The demon came out and a fierce fight broke between the two. The prince cut his right hand. Seeing this, other demons also started attacking the prince. But no weapon did any harm to the prince. The crystal eye had made him invincible. He slayed all the evil demons and freed his people. He was told that his father, the King was still alive and kept in the dungeons. He freed the King and restored him to the throne and there was happiness all over!"

***

His mother would have told him the same story upteenth times. He was always happier listening to the story. The good always prevails over evil at the end. God is always just. He was sure that his mother would also feel better listening to the story.

Reciting the story in that detail for a four-year-old is unusual. But that wasn't the only unusual thing about him. His physique, fearlessness, mental alertness and inquisitiveness were far ahead of his peers. On the upper right arm, he had a birthmark just like that of his father. He had not seen that on other kids. The birthmark which resembled an eye, made him different from others and he felt proud of it. Many a times, he found elders touching his birthmark in reverence. Two mothers had also come with their infants and touched his birthmark to seek blessings.

Vikram did enjoy these, but he also felt a great sense of responsibility.

He looked at his mother's face. She smiled but tears started rolling down her cheeks.

"Is the story real, mother?"

"Let us sleep now," his mother said with a smile that appeared somewhat defeated. She held him tight as they tried to sleep. And a tired Vikram was thinking as he dozed off, "How can a mother like this be cursed?"

It is said that the Bhola cyclone of 1970 wreaked havoc in the Bay of Bengal. Killing almost 300-500,000 people in the erstwhile East Pakistan, it was the deadliest tropical cyclone ever recorded. It was also one of the deadliest natural disasters of all times.

The North Sentinel Island, 36km west of South Andaman and 50km west of Port Blair, saw catastrophic devastation. Completely secluded from the rest of the world, the dense forest did play the role of its name and managed to save a couple of caves, but most of the few hundred already creaking hamlets were too weak to withstand the fury of the cyclone Bhola.

❊ ❊ ❊

Chapter 13
Brick Kiln of Cooch Behar

A few years later at Cooch Behar on the India-Bangladesh border…

"Hey, you come here!"

The fat bald owner of the brick kiln shouted at one of the women standing in the queue to receive her daily wage from the accountant. "You are still short of moving ten bricks! Go first, do your work and then come back!"

The frail looking woman in her forties had her face hidden inside her saree. She raised her head towards the kiln owner. Although she knew that she had completed her work, she took the basket and went towards the kiln. It was already getting dark. As she moved away from the men and women in the queue, suddenly a policeman came in front of her.

He came close to her. His mouth smelling of liquor was almost touching her face. His smile was as disgusting as the stains on his teeth. She quickly closed her nose with her hands and tried to shove him away from her.

"How dare you push a policeman?" he somehow fumbled still unable to stand firm on his feet.

"Please let me go. I have not done anything," cried the woman.

The policeman caught hold of her arm. "Don't you know what have you done? You have stolen my heart. I have not been able to sleep since the time I have seen you. Come with me for a night. I will make you a queen!"

He tried to drag the woman inside the darkness of the nearby field.

"Help! Please leave me alone! Someone please help me!"

The cries were loud. Whether they missed the few of the laborers still waiting in the queue or they just chose to ignore as it was a common sight there, it was not clear. As the woman struggled, a strong hand gripped the policeman from behind. The grip on the neck was so strong that the policeman could not utter a word. His eyes almost popped out. He was drunk and out of his senses. He quickly fell onto the ground. Vikram hit him hard in the stomach. Just one punch made him unconscious.

Vikram could have killed him but his mother pulled him away. "Come, son! If we kill him, then we will not be able to live in peace ever."

Vikram's eyes were red, partly from anger and partly from his inability to help mother. His head remained bowed.

"Come fast now, dear. We will need to leave this place soon. The policeman will wake up and try to find us. It appears that the kiln owner was also hand-in-gloves with him. He will not give us work. We will need to move to another place."

In the past seven years after they had left the North Sentinel Island and reached India via Bangladesh, they had come across several humiliating experiences. They had struggled to keep themselves alive. They had no legitimate papers for citizenship which made them very vulnerable. At times, they had to sleep empty stomach. Every now and then, they had to be on the move.

Vikram's mother had no formal education. But having grown up in the jungle, her sixth sense was very strong. She could sense changes in the weather beforehand. She knew a lot about herbs and wild vegetation which could be used to cure various diseases as well as provide strength to the body.

As a result, despite lack of sufficient resources, she was able to give Vikram a nutritious diet most of the times. At eleven years of age, Vikram easily equaled a man in his early twenties. The rough life had helped him develop a strong built. None of the kids could beat him in any of the sports.

Vikram's mother had also got old school books which others would discard at times. She understood that life in this jungle of humans was even tougher than the one back at the North Sentinel Island. It was important to study and learn various traits. Lacking proper citizenship papers and adequate funds, they were often forced to move. Though unable to attend school, Vikram studied whatever he could find. He was remarkably sharp.

Vikram and his mother left the place immediately. The policeman had been stalking Vikram's mother since quite some time. She had spurned his advances somehow. Now that the policeman has hurt, she knew that as soon as he woke up, he would come along with other policemen looking for them. Their lack of citizenship papers anyway made them vulnerable.

They picked up their belongings. It had already become dark. Leaving the village in dark would not be safe. They were in two minds when an old lady staying the next door came in.

"I heard what happened today. My son has another house at the outskirts. He uses it only for storage in the harvesting season. If you want, you can stay there till the morning and then leave in the wee hours."

The lady was very old and suffered from arthritis. Vikram's mother had created some ointment for relieving her pain and the old lady wanted to help them in this hour of need.

Vikram took the key. They covered themselves from head to toe and quickly walked towards the house. On their way out, they heard few men talking in hushed tones. They slowed down to catch their conversation.

"Did you hear what happened at the kiln today?"

"I did. But I think it served the policeman right. After all, he had been casting evil eyes on several of the women in the village."

"True. In fact, he even teased young girls several times."

"He got what he deserved at last!"

"But I am worried what may happen now! After his murder, other policemen will not leave Vikram and his mother alive. Who knows if they might vent their anger on us?"

"And where did Vikram get hold of such a dagger? It looked quite expensive! Someone was telling it had a beautiful eye crafted on it."

Vikram and his mother hastened their steps. Their heartbeats had increased. Next day early morning, they saw a bullock cart going out of the village. They got on it.

Vikram's mother had not slept the whole night. She was very tired.

He took her head in his lap. "Take some rest now, mother. Everything will be alright. Let me tell you the story of the crystal eye."

❁ ❁ ❁

Chapter 14

Misfortune Continues to Follow

The hot and humid weather of Calcutta was even more punishing. Days of journey, at times on foot, and not much money to spare had weakened them.

"It is so strange. Those who do not have much, are ready to share whatever they have. And those who have, not only ignore the problems of others but are ready to pounce and weaken you further." Vikram's mother said to him as they moved in an old and damp hut that an old lady offered to them for as long as they stayed.

They were starving but happy that no one appeared to be chasing them. As Vikram put his mother to sleep, he started thinking of how to earn money so that they could survive. The next day, the hut owner took him to a newspaper shop. One of his helpers had left for the village and had not returned since long. The owner was old and wanted a reliable hand to distribute newspapers in the morning to the neighborhood.

As Vikram bowed in front of him, the owner looked at him from top to bottom. "Will you be able to wake up early in the morning? The van brings the papers here by 5 am and then we have to make bunches for delivery in various areas. By 6 am, you must deliver the newspaper. That is the first thing that people want in the morning. If you delay, they will change to someone else."

With folded hands, Vikram said, "Yes dada. I will come on time. You will not be disappointed."

"Ok then, come tomorrow by 5 am here."

The next day, the old shop owner gave him an old bike in the morning. With a bundle of newspaper on the carrier of the bike, he happily rode off to the addresses mentioned in the list.

Vikram was really happy that he had started earning something. Slowly, one of his clients also employed him for small jobs. Mostly, Vikram used to drop his five-year kid Daksh to the school around two kilometers away, bring him back home and play with him for some time.

Vikram's mother had also started working as a helper in a nearby grocery store.

Life was going well.

Vikram used to read newspaper in his free time. He had befriended a teacher in Daksh's school. Whatever he did not understand, he would circle that out and ask Daksh's teacher.

Yes, life did appear going well until that night…

It was a Sunday. The grocery store where his mother used to work was closed. After a long walk with friends, Vikram was returning in the evening when he saw a small crowd at the hut where he was staying with his mother.

He quickly ran towards the hut.

"She must have fallen hard."

"Doesn't look as if she is alive."

"Where is Vikram? We need to take her to the doctor."

He heard those voices as he stepped inside the hut to find her mother lying in a pool of blood on the floor.

He quickly checked the pulse and was relieved to find that his mother was still alive. Her right temple seemed to be hurt. He quickly grabbed a piece of cloth and wrapped her head tightly.

With the help of few men, he laid her down on a cot. They then took him to the nearest doctor available.

He knocked hard on the door of the doctor. By that time, it was almost 10pm. Vikram was sweating profusely. He did not want to lose his mother. After all, she was the only one left with him. He had lost his father. When he left North Sentinel Island along with his mother, he had also left behind whoever was alive after the deadly Bhola cyclone had swept the Island.

More importantly, he had always seen his mother struggling. Back at the island, when everything was going well, despite being the wife of the headman, she was almost ostracized by the community. While he and his father were welcomed everywhere, hardly anyone spoke to her. In hushed tones, he had heard several times "She is a curse!"

It was late at night. Just before it appeared as if the door would come off, someone hurriedly came down and opened the door from inside the house.

"What is it? Why are you breaking my door?" The doctor spoke in an angry voice.

"I am sorry, doctor. My mother is bleeding. I am not sure what happened. When I came home, I saw her in a pool of blood. Her head seems to have been hit by something. I have wrapped a cloth there to stop the blood but it hasn't stopped bleeding. Please tend to her." Vikram almost begged with folded hands to the doctor.

A crowd of 15-20 people had gathered by that time. Most were there just to witness the event than to offer any kind of help. One elderly woman stepped ahead to request the doctor, "She is a nice woman and they have always helped us. Please be kind to her, doctor. She has lost a lot of blood. Please treat her!"

"What can I do? Take her to the hospital. I am already tired and I do not even have the equipment at home to treat such a wound," said the doctor. It was a small locality and the doctor was pissed off with Vikram's mother who had started driving his patients away with her knowledge of herbal medicines. It was payback time for him.

Helpless Vikram aware of the precious time being lost swung ahead and caught hold of the doctor's neck. "Look doctor! We have had enough! If you do not treat her right away, I will…"

His voice was drowned in the wailing sounds of an ambulance which screeched to halt near them. The back door opened fast and two men came down with a stretcher. They quickly started lifting Vikram's mother from the cot onto the stretcher.

"Who are you?" Vikram asked those men.

"We are from a nearby hospital. Please come along with us. We have been sent to bring your mother. Come and sit inside. We will treat her and she will be alright."

Vikram was puzzled. But there was nothing better that he could have wished for. He climbed onto the ambulance. The ambulance moved ahead fast and within minutes reached a small hospital. A doctor was waiting there. He soon did a quick inspection.

"Bring the saline bottle quickly and check her blood type," he ordered the nurse standing nearby. One person set up the saline while another took out her blood sample. In the meanwhile, the doctor cleaned up her wound and put up a bandage over it.

"Thank God that you brought her here in time. She has lost a lot of blood. But she will be fine soon as we infuse some blood and medicines. Do not worry, Vikram. She will be fine. And do not worry about money. We will take care of everything," said the doctor.

Vikram bowed with folded hands. A stream of tears ran down his face. The doctor patted his back. Vikram was glad that his mother was being taken care of. But he was also very confused. Although he used to deliver newspaper in the vicinity, he had not come this far ever. Who had sent for the ambulance? How on earth did the doctor know his name? He and his mother were poor. They could definitely not afford such a good medical facility. In such a selfish world, why was the doctor not asking for any money? And most importantly, how did his mother get hurt? They did not have enmity with anyone!

Thinking of all these, the thirteen-year-old Vikram dozed off in the chair beside his mother in the hospital. A couple of patients lay in that big shared room.

He suddenly felt a strong wave of heat almost burning his eyes. He woke up to find that there was fire everywhere. He was unable to understand what had happened. He checked on his mother. Her eyes were open. She tried to mutter something in a feeble voice. People were running here and there. He could not see where the door was. From whatever little he could see through; he saw a group of people with swords and other arms running inside the hospital.

Someone threw a large stone which landed beside him. He did not know what to do. The armed men were running after those left in the hospital. Whosoever came within their reach was not spared. He quickly took a look around to see that not even the patients were left alive. Cries for help and loud screams kept coming from behind the cloak of smoke.

Those men were coming near fast. Vikram did not understand what to do. He could have run away but how could he leave his mother behind? With her and fire all around, it was difficult to go much far. He did not even know where to go.

Suddenly, he felt the sound of metal clashing against metal just behind his ear. He turned around to see that a person almost attacked him with a sword. However, another person with a slight limp had countered that with an iron rod. The man with the limp then thrust a dagger inside the belly of the attacker, twisted it and pulled it out. Despite the whole chaos and violence, Vikram did not fail to notice that the dagger had a distinct eye made on its handle. He had a sense as if he had heard about it in the past.

"Go away, Vikram. Take your mother on your back. Leave fast. Go from behind. There is a blue color van standing there. It does not have a number plate. They will keep you safe. Run fast!"

The limping man then snatched the sword from another attacker. He kicked him at his temple and the attacker fell on the ground immediately. Seeing him fall, two other men came materialized from somewhere. Vikram lifted his mother in his arms and ran in the direction as directed. As his mother's head was near his own, he felt his mother wanted to say something but he could barely hear anything amidst violence all around. He said, "Do not worry mother. We will all be safe. I will take care of you."

As he lowered his head to caress his mother, she managed to utter few broken words, "The eye…the story of the crystal eye is real…go and find it…and take its blessings!"

He could not understand what she was speaking. Moreover, it was not a time to think but to act fast and save their lives. He turned back to see that his rescuer had been holding the attackers well. There were in fact four men now fighting against him. But despite the limp, the man appeared much stronger than all of them.

As he came out, he found a blue van right in front of him. The otherwise dark street was also lit brightly in the fury of violence. Many parts of the street were up in smoke. Shops had been vandalized. Houses had been broken into. There was no one on the street. It appeared as if death was patrolling the street looking for victims!

"Come inside, Vikram!" The driver of the blue van shouted at him. Vikram had never seen this driver before. But there was hardly any choice in front of him. He laid his mother on the seat and sat beside her.

Outside, the street was burning. Vikram had a lot of questions. What had just happened? How did so many people he had never met know him? Were these rioters after Vikram and his mother? Why did these few men risk their lives to save them?

As the van screeched away from the hospital, he felt the need for the answers. But he knew he had to allow the driver to concentrate on his driving so that they could reach a safe place. As the van moved away, he saw the limping man come out from the hospital with a sword in each of his arms.

Vikram was glad that the man was safe. "What just happened in this area?" he asked the driver.

You know, the local election is coming up," the driver said. "Here, people from one political party see those from other parties as enemies. They're even willing to kill each other over politics!"

Even as the driver was speaking, Vikram saw a small group of people chasing a white car in front of him. The driver of his van sped up in order to overtake and leave the group behind. But someone threw a petrol bomb which landed inside the van. There was a loud explosion and the van hit the white car. Vikram's hand was injured. He fell out of the van. He looked ahead to see that a sword had pierced his driver's stomach. His head had swung on one side. He quickly ran to check on his mother. Her eyes were closed. He checked her pulse. There was none. He tried to press her chest to see if he could revive her. But he somehow knew that his efforts were futile. Someone pulled him from the burning van. By the time he fell outside, the van was engulfed in fire. The van exploded with a loud noise. He saw people running here and there. He tried to look back. The van looked nothing but a loose assembly of burnt metal.

His whole world had fallen apart. The white car had hit the pavement. The door was open. That driver had also been murdered.

As Vikram tried to move away from there, the body of a boy fell from the white car. Vikram was unable to understand how people could be so cruel to each other. He had lost his mother. The street was deserted. He just sat on the pavement crying at what he had just gone through. Tears came out like a large dam had just broken down. But there was no sound.

The van was still burning with his mother inside it. At last, her suffering was over. A barrage of images flashed in front of his eyes. When he was a kid way back at his island, he would run in the jungle and hide somewhere and his mother would come from behind and surprise him. She would lift him high in the sky and they would play all day long. She was so happy with him and his father around. He did not remember seeing her sad. Except when sometimes, someone would comment that she was cursed. His mother would never reply back, but she definitely appeared hurt. But now everything had come to an end.

There was no one on the empty street. He did not know what to do. He was deep in his thoughts when he felt as if he heard a feeble voice. The van had been burnt down completely. He looked around. He looked towards the white car. He saw the hand of the boy moving.

Vikram quickly rushed to the boy. "Please help me!" the boy muttered in a feeble voice. He appeared a few years younger than Vikram. His leg was stuck inside the car and there were bruises all over his body. One of his arms was dangling outside the car while the other had been torn off. The wound was bleeding.

His mother was dead. Life was about to change forever. From where did so many people who knew him emerge all of a sudden? His oldest and strongest relationship had come to an end. And a whole new chapter was about to begin. What did future have in store for him?

❁ ❁ ❁

Chapter 15
The Fight at Sita Kund

Almost two decades later…1996…the last year…in Munger…

Bang. Bang. The loud sound of the two-gun shots could be heard despite the noise of the crowd inside the Sita Kund temple. People ducked for cover wherever they could. Amid the rustle and bustle of almost a thousand of people gathered there for the annual fare, three men inside the temple threw their shawls up in the air shouting the crowd to leave the temple immediately.

"Run away quickly. We are not here to hurt you. Just leave the temple immediately."

There were only a handful of priests inside the sanctum sanctorum preparing for the morning rituals. Even before they could come out, the two men stood before them at the gate of the temple. Amid the chaos outside the temple, a jeep screeched to a stop outside the main gate. There was a total of six men inside. They all had rifles in their hands, except the driver. Three men jumped from the jeep and walked slowly to the sanctum sanctorum. Despite the fact that the crowd outnumbered them, no one dared to challenge them. Most just ran away, falling, getting hurt and then rising again to save their lives.

The men were too audacious. They had not even covered their faces. They joined the three men who had shot the bullets in the air earlier.

They took their sandals off before entering the sanctum sanctorum. Two men each stood as guards at the two doors while the other two men went inside. "Do not panic. We are not here to hurt you. Where is Nirmala?" It was winter and the five priests had covered themselves with shawls. Two of them had covered their heads as well. Only their eyes were visible.

One of the men shouted again, "Where is Nirmala? We just want her. All others can go. Tell us quickly or we will break your bones."

Most priests were trembling with fear. One of them clutched the hand of another tightly. One of the priests mustered some courage. Stammering badly, he asked, "Why are you looking for her? What has she done?"

"We do not know. Our boss has asked to bring her to him."

The priests did not know what to say. One of them asked, "Who is your boss? Why does he want Nirmala? What has she done?"

One of the men thrust the nozzle of his rifle at the throat of that priest. "Just hand us Nirmala. Or we will ransack the whole temple and take her anyway. Don't make it difficult for you. You do not know who we..."

Even before he could complete his sentence, shawl of one of the priests fell onto the ground and suddenly the man felt a strong kick on his chin. Before he could even absorb the extent to which he was hurt, another kick from the same priest landed on the chest of the other man holding the rifle. Both fell down writhing in pain. They tried looking up. In a cool demeanor, Nirmala had lifted a rifle from the ground. Hearing their friends in pain, all four men tried coming inside. There was hardly any space inside. Even as they tried, Nirmala pushed the two men coming from the right-side door.

Apparently, the men had not anticipated any resistance. The two men, who were kicked inside the temple, got up slowly. Along with the others, they ran after her. But Nirmala was much faster than them. One of them immediately rushed back inside the sanctum sanctorum and held the neck of one of the priests. "Nirmala! Do not run away. Or else, I will kill this old man…"

Nirmala stopped and turned around. She was holding the rifle in her hand. Without saying a word, she started returning with very slow and calibrated steps. She saw one of the six men holding an old priest by his neck. Another of these men was pointing his rifle at his chest. Other four men were standing on the left.

As she came almost within their reach, the four men started to move to catch hold of her. Nirmala was still few steps away. She dropped her rifle. Suddenly, she ran at her full speed. Within no time, a strong flying kick hit the man who held the old priest hostage. The rifle fell from his hands. As Nirmala landed on the ground, another roundabout kick landed on the one that was holding the priest's neck.

The kick had landed on his ear. Both of the men fell to the ground instantly. The other four men were completely shocked to see such a fierce fight from Nirmala.

In that part of the world, females were considered to be physically weaker. And a lean and thin girl fighting armed men stunned them. They did not know how to react. They just stood there in silence for few moments. One of them then shouted for help. The other three in the jeep jumped down and rushed to the spot. Nirmala was still standing there calmly. The old priest had run away inside. Nirmala asked, "Why are you after me? I have not harmed anyone. Go away from here!" Her voice was firm.

The men then formed a circle around her. She was outnumbered one to nine. She did not know if there were others hidden elsewhere. She had dropped the rifle that she had snatched. She was very alert.

One of the men said, "Our boss saw you somewhere. He has sent us to fetch for you. Come with us. Else, we will take you by force."

Nirmala shuffled her legs and quickly mounted a side kick on the one standing on her left. He fell down immediately. Without wasting any time, Nirmala then lifted her back leg and kicked another one on his chin hard. The others came nearer to overpower her. She hit the nearest one on his face with her elbow. The punch was so hard that he started bleeding. By that time, another one had come closer to her and aimed his rifle at her back. Although she tried to duck, she could not move so fast and the butt of his rifle ended up hitting her ribs. She cried out in pain and fell on the ground clutching her ribs. The crowd had already dispersed from the temple. Those who could not, were hiding like cowards behind nooks and corners. No one came for help. Another of those men quickly took out a handkerchief and put it on Nirmala's face. The sweet-smelling chloroform made her unconscious immediately.

❁ ❁ ❁

Chapter 16

The Man from Bardah

Nirmala was knocked out completely. The men lifted her to the jeep. There was still no one who came to help her. They hurriedly placed her at the back seat of the jeep and rode off. The jeep kept going for almost an hour. The road was smooth so far. Nirmala was still unconscious. Suddenly, the jeep took an off beaten track. It appeared as if there was no road at all, only sand and dust everywhere. The jeep shook badly. But the jerking motions were also helping Nirmala in gaining her consciousness back.

After almost half an hour riding through what appeared like an unpaved road, Nirmala felt her nerves coming back. She was still weak. "I am not fit enough to fight so many men," she thought. She kept her eyes closed. After a while, she felt the jeep stopping near a deserted area. She was huddled at the back seat. But now she felt as if the jeep had more space. Probably few people had gotten off. After few minutes, one of the men said, "The chloroform was quite strong. She would not be awake for another two hours."

"What a fight she put! Now I know why brother is after her!" said another one. "You two can also get down here. We three can take her to my brother," he continued.

"So there are only three men now," said Nirmala to herself. She opened her eyes slightly to confirm. The jerks had already shaken off most of the unconsciousness. The situation presented by fewer men got her nerves back as well. Her floating ribs were still aching. But her steely determination provided them extra strength. Two men were standing at the back with her while the other was driving.

She quickly put her arm around the neck of the man nearer to her and kicked the other man in the groin hard. He collapsed. Her grip on the other man's neck was so tight that he could not even breathe. She stretched her arm and suddenly hit his temple with her knuckle with almost clinical precision. As the man fell down, she could see a line of blood trickling down his nose. He stopped moving.

The driver was stunned with the commotion at the back. He turned around to see what was happening forgetting how bad the road was. His hands came off the steering and the jeep swerved to the left only to hit a boulder. With a bang, the jeep came to a halt. Nirmala had already jumped off the jeep. The left part of the jeep had buckled in with the impact. The driver had been thrown off. She saw that the two men on the jeep were still not getting up. She turned around. The driver got up and took out a sharp small knife and was hurling abuses at her. But he kept himself at a cautious distance. He was throwing the knife from one hand to the other and challenging her.

Nirmala stood still. She started moving towards the driver. He was now really scared. He had already seen that if they had not hit her with the butt of the rifle from the back, even all nine of them were no match for her. He stepped back. He knew that he could not even run away. His boss would not leave him alive for such a botched-up operation. He suddenly ran towards Nirmala with full force and tried to hit her hard with the knife. She just took a step aside and let him fall on the jeep. The knife fell with full force on the tank of the jeep. He had hit the tank really hard which was already weak from the impact when the jeep had crashed. Drops of diesel started trickling down from the already damaged fuel tank. The man lost his balance and fell down. As he started to find balance, he felt a sharp kick on his head. A roundhouse kick and Nirmala's ball of feet landed on his forehead knocking him down. He was motionless. Nirmala then turned to the two men at the back of the jeep. The one, who was bleeding from his nose, was still motionless. The other was still coiled, hands clutched at his aching groin. He raised his head looking at Nirmala. His dilated pupils spoke of fear.

Nirmala came nearer. Seeing death in front of him, his guts gave out, making his pants wet. Tears started rolling down his cheeks. "Forgive me please! Let me go!"

"Why are you all after me?"

"My brother asked to bring you to him. He saw you somewhere. I don't know why. We were just following his orders."

"Who is your brother? What is his name? Where does he live?" Nirmala asked, never once raising her voice. She was still very poised, as if the whole event was no great a challenge to her. She knew her capabilities well. These men were nothing. They could not harm her in anyway.

"His name is Vikram and we are from Bardah village."

"Don't you have girls at Bardah? Why is he after me? Why didn't he come himself?"

She vaguely remembered reading about the village in the local newspaper some time back. The village was notorious for arms peddling. The article said that a bunch of men had been captured there just weeks ago. They were smuggling few AK-47 rifles. She knew that if she left him conscious, he could try to contact his brother and his gang. She was not sure where exactly she was. What if more of the gang came for her? She was exhausted. Could she fight more people? What if they came with arms? Some of these villages were very notorious. She could find herself against hundred odd men. The best was to return safely to her home. Vikram could be dealt with later.

She leaned towards the man. He raised his hand to save himself. "Normally, I do not hit a half dead person like you," said Nirmala. She suddenly brought down the side of her hand hard on his neck. It was just below his ear. The man became motionless immediately. She had hit the area that contained the carotid artery, jugular vein and Vagus nerve. He would not die, but would not wake up for a couple of hours. That would give her sufficient time to go far away.

❀ ❀ ❀

Chapter 17

Preparing for the Fare at Sita Kund

The present day…1997…

Rakesh asked his friend Shakti, "Are you also going to Sita Kund for the annual fare?" Shakti nodded in affirmative. Few months ago, the chief priest of Sita Kund had come to meet one of the priests at the Kashtaharni Ghat temple. He had come to seek support for organizing the annual fare at Sita Kund. Over the years, the annual fare had been witnessing much more crowd. As the number of devotees increased, so did the traders who came to display their wood works. The two fed on each other and since last two years, they were witnessing more than five thousand devotees daily.

"Have to. We have formed a committee of six priests and have even enrolled nine devotees. We have divided ourselves into three sub groups- each having two priests and three devotees. Each sub group would go there on a rotating basis daily. We leave early morning and return the next day morning from there," said Shakti.

"I was wondering why they require help from here! I am sure that they would have a large contingent of priests there itself. Since the crowd has increased, I am sure that they could enroll more devotees to take care of the arrangements," said Rakesh a bit puzzled.

Shakti replied, "During the discussions, I think I also heard someone mentioning that there was some law and order problem last year. Since the district administrator lives in this area, the priests here have much better contact with them. It is much easier to get support from the local police if we request them rather than talking to them directly. In fact, there is a small contingent of 5-6 policemen guarding the temple premises. They have been stationed there to avoid any untoward incident."

Sita Kund is a small temple in Munger, a small town on the banks of Holy Ganges. The legend says that when Lord Rama returned from Lanka after killing Raavana, he asked Sita to prove her chastity by walking through a pyre of fire. It is said that Sita walked through the fire and then took her bath in a nearby pond. The pond has remained hot ever since, unable to absorb the heat from Sita's body.

In fact, there are four more ponds nearby each bearing the name of the four brothers- Rama, Bharat, Laxman and Shatrughna. The water in these ponds is at ambient temperature and the water inside Sita Kund is the only one which is hot. There have been several studies but no one has been able to find out the reason.

The temple hosts an annual fare in the month of February. It goes on for a few days. The area around the temple hosts various kinds of traders, mostly who trade in wood products including furniture.

It was almost eight months ago that the chief priest of Sita Kund had come to seek support from the priests at the Kashtaharni Ghat temple. The three friends, Binod, Rakesh and Shakti were also present briefly when the discussion was going on.

"I am going there tomorrow. Why don't you also come along? It will be quite fun together," said Shakti.

Rakesh was looking for an excuse to go there anyway. He happily nodded, "Sure!"

Chapter 18

The Annual Fair at Sita Kund

They had come across this girl when they were exploring Mir Qasim's Tunnel. The first encounter at Sita Kund had made Rakesh very nervous and Nirmala very embarrassed. After all, he had emerged from nowhere into Rama Kund when she was taking her bath. He feared that she might find out about what they were looking at and Nirmala was embarrassed as she had not anticipated anyone there when she was taking her bath, although with her clothes on.

He got another chance to see her when the chief priest of Sita Kund, her father, came along with her to the Kashtaharni Ghat to seek support for this year's annual fair. He had not forgotten her big and misty eyes. He had wanted to meet her again ever since. He had visited Sita Kund without telling his friends twice but could not see her. He was very excited now. With the annual fare ongoing, there was no chance of missing her!

The next day, he reached Kashtaharni Ghat early in the morning at 5:30 am. The group of two priests and three devotees had hired a van to go to Sita Kund. "Come at the back, Rakesh," said Shakti. It took them around half an hour to reach Sita Kund. It was not that far away. But the road was not so good and there was hardly any streetlight. February was cold in Munger and it was still quite dark without the streetlights.

As they reached, the group of earlier priests and devotees were already waiting outside the temple. Shakti said jokingly, "You still look fresh! Hope everything was alright yesterday." After brief conversation on the arrangements, the earlier group boarded the same van and returned. As they were entering the temple premises, they heard someone ring the temple bell. It was still dark although dawn had started to break in. Under the faint light of the bulb on the pole nearby, they saw the silhouette of a girl moving out of the temple. She was still facing the temple.

Rakesh's heart started pacing. Was it the same girl that he had met inside the Sita Kund last year? Was it the same girl that he had gone twice to see but could not meet? That too without even informing his childhood friends! Was it the one who kept coming in his dreams ever since he had seen her?

Drowning in his thoughts, he did not even realize when the girl went past him. "Stop staring!" Nirmala said in a low voice as she passed behind Rakesh. The others did not hear.

She folded her hands and said, "Good morning, gentlemen. Thanks for coming. I have prepared tea and snacks for you. Please wait inside that room. I will come and serve you in a minute. Please eat properly. Later, it would be difficult to find time as devotees start pouring in." She then left..

The group was delighted with the warm welcome. They proceeded towards the room. Shakti realized that Rakesh was still standing there itself. "What happened? Come here fast Rakesh! We do not have much time. There is a lot of work to do."

Along with other three, he took the charge of security at the main gate. There was a temporary arrangement made to make devotees stand in a queue at the entrance. He saw that there were two policemen standing and shouting at people for the same. He also saw two policemen just outside the sanctum sanctorum. The ones outside had rifles. The ones inside just had long sticks. Probably firearms were not allowed inside the temple, he thought. He also saw two more men roaming outside in the area where the vendors had put up their stalls.

There was no X-ray machine or any hand-held device even at the main entrance. They were just asking devotees to open their bags to check what lay inside. He was not sure how effective that was. But he saw that the bags were being checked very seriously. Even if they found a matchbox, the devotees were asked to throw that outside. There was a lot of commotion, but the guards were insisting for a thorough check. At times, they also ran their hands over the devotees to check if they were hiding anything. He remembered how one policeman had guided him about doing these checks just moments back when he was having his breakfast.

He had come across more stringent checks at other places that he had visited in the past. He was not sure what the reason for such stringent checks was. But then he remembered that there had been some law and order problem last year. Probably that triggered the security this time, he thought.

The crowd kept surging in the morning. But as the heat increased with the day time, there was a slowdown in the stream of devotees. At times, he and three others at the main gate security were just waiting for someone to come. "This is the right moment to ask these men," he thought.

"Dada, do we get similar large crowds every year?" he was being cautious so that his questioning did not raise any suspicion.

"Almost, it has been increasing every year."

"It is such a difficult task to handle such large flow of devotees! I have come here earlier but never during the annual fare. At few other temples, I have seen administration using automatic X-ray machines to scan bags. But those are more vulnerable with large number of outstation tourists. I know that this temple has its own identity with the legends of Sita around it. But we still do not see outstation tourists. Mostly, devotees are from nearby villages only. I am sure that if we start asking around, we would hardly find anyone who does not know anyone else participating in the fare."

"True, most people are from nearby villages. They belong to local communities only."

"Then what exactly is the purpose of such strict checking? I am sure that it would be difficult for anyone to create trouble hear without getting caught."

"What you're saying is true. Till last year, we did not have such elaborate security arrangement. We did force devotees to come in a queue. But we never used to open and search their bags. But then last year, we had an untoward incident."

Rakesh became more eager to know. "What happened?"

But then, the men got busy with few more devotees that had come.

It was almost 1pm. "Gentlemen, please take these lunch boxes and keep eating one by one as you get time. The crowd will again surge in few hours. If you need anything else, please do let me know," he found Nirmala standing in front of them. Nirmala went back as quickly as she had come. Rakesh had been wanting to talk to her. He knew that today was a lucky day. He might not get another chance sooner.

"Come, Rakesh. Let us finish our lunch till the time these two take care of things here," one of the men said, interrupting the thought that Rakesh was occupied with. He went aside with that person to have the lunch.

"Dada, the food is very delicious! I wish I could come here tomorrow as well!" The other person laughed.

"I hope we do not come across any incident like that in the last year. I don't want to take any risk."

"Was it so bad last year? What happened?"

"A gang of men had come from some village to abduct Nirmala. She put up a brave fight but I hear that they had succeeded in kidnapping her. But then same day, she came back home by the evening. She had few bruises here and there. The jeep that they had used to abduct her was found charred later on several kilometers away from here. Four men were also found almost burnt fully to death. There was some investigation. It was found that three of the men who had died belonged to the group that had abducted Nirmala. No one knows about who the fourth person was. They also found a bottle of alcohol nearby."

Rakesh's head was almost spinning with what he had learned. Someone had tried to abduct Nirmala last year? He felt his fists clenching and his lower jaw pressing up against the upper jaw in anger. His eyes had narrowed. Not that he knew much about Nirmala. But she looked so innocent a person! Why would anyone want to harm her?

The other person realized that Rakesh was not listening any more. "Where are you lost Rakesh? Finish your lunch quickly so that the other two can also have their lunch."

Rakesh quickly gobbled the food. He was no longer smiling. He knew that the whole city of Munger itself was notorious for illegal gun making factories and arms trade. The city had the honor of hosting the first ever gun making factory when the British had come. But slowly, the factory closed down. With the closure, so many skilled laborers were left without work. Most of them knew nothing except gun making. It was easy for them to fall into wrong hands. Numerous illegal shops mushroomed in the remote corners under the tutelage of powerful but criminal elements of the society. Not that the police was not aware. But who does not enjoy a few extra bucks!

He wanted to know more. But if he asked others, people would unnecessarily notice him. Why was a person so interested in what had happened last year when others were not talking about it?

He decided to keep quiet and do some research himself. He saw Nirmala a couple of times more in the day. She was busy in temple arrangements. They did not talk much. It was difficult for Rakesh to pass the day now. But when the crowd surged around 4pm, he became alert. He now understood the gravity of the threat. He did not want anyone to hurt Nirmala anymore. Suddenly, he was feeling very protective about her. He did not know why.

By around 9 pm, the crowd had thinned. Few of the policemen had gone away. Vendors had almost shut their shops. There were hardly a handful of devotees inside the temple premises. Rakesh had returned to the room along with another of the guys. He found Shakti waiting for him.

"So how was the day, Rakesh?" For the whole day, Shakti had been confined to the sanctum sanctorum. He was assisting the chief priest in performing various rituals.

"Very tiring." He wanted to share with Shakti whatever he had learnt. After all, they were very good friends since childhood. But there were too many people there. He could wait.

"Thank you very much for your help today. We will bring your dinner in few minutes," the chief priest came along with Nirmala to the room. He continued "I know it is a bit difficult to adjust so many of you in this small room. But we are constrained this season. From next time onwards, we will prepare for a better experience for the volunteers."

"Absolutely not! This is perfect, Pandit ji. It is winter anyway," said one of the several men who had come from outside to help them. Apart from the group from Kashtaharni Ghat, apparently there were few more from distant temples.

By the time they had finished their dinner, it was pretty cold. All men were tired from standing throughout the day. Rakesh and Shakti were sleeping close to each other. But

Rakesh was unable to sleep. He was still thinking about last year's incident.

"Shakti, have you slept?" whispered Rakesh amidst sounds of snoring from a few people inside the room. There was no response from Shakti. He was hard asleep. Rakesh sighed and closed his eyes.

❁ ❁ ❁

Chapter 19

The Friends Discover More About the Previous Year

Rakesh woke up the next morning with the sound of the temple bell. The next batch of volunteers had come to replace them. He returned along with the group which had come from Kashtaharni Ghat.

In the evening, Rakesh went to the Sri Krishna Library to check. He went to the newspaper section and started taking out older issues. He focused on local newspapers. These would be small incidents and probably covered well in local editions.

He started from 1st February 1996. He searched one local newspaper date wise. In the 14th February 1996 print, he found a mention of abduction from Sita Kund. The vernacular had mentioned how in a daring event, a group of nine men had kidnapped Nirmala, the daughter of the chief priest from Sita Kund. It described the incident in some detail. It was mentioned that the lean girl fought off the gang well. But no one came out to help. Finally, they overpowered her and took her on a jeep. The chief priest had filed a case in the local police station. On the next day's edition, it was mentioned at the back somewhere that Nirmala had returned to the temple. The jeep in which she had been kidnapped was found charred completely. There were four burnt corpses. Not much was written in this small piece of coverage.

He searched the same newspaper for few subsequent days' coverage. Almost a week later, there was a small article which had mentioned that the police had concluded that three of the corpses belonged to Vikram's gang. They had not found anything about the fourth corpse. The police had found a bottle of alcohol nearby. The police had concluded further that the fourth person was drunk. He had come in front of the vehicle because of which the vehicle lost balance and hit a boulder. It got damaged and caught fire, immediately killing all four men. One of them was also the younger brother of Vikram. There was no mention of Nirmala in this article.

Rakesh searched for a few more days. One of the articles mentioned that the police had raided Bardah village. This was in relation to an older case involving smuggling of AK-47. Vikram, the supposed kingpin, had been able to run away from the place though.

Rakesh also searched another newspaper for clues. But he could not find anything more. He quickly took those newspapers out and got a photo copy of those relevant articles.

The next day, he met Shakti. "Boy, this is interesting! I did not know that so much had happened last year. But even more importantly, I am unable to understand why are you taking so much interest?" asked Shakti with a smirk on his face.

Rakesh smiled, "It is nothing. From the day that I saw her last year, somehow, she keeps coming before me."

"Or, you keep finding reasons to go in front of her," chuckled Shakti. Both laughed.

"You and Binod are the only two friends I have. I do not want to hide anything. I do like her very much. And now that I have discovered all this, I want to make sure that at least she is safe. It appears that he is in hiding. But the threat is still looming. Else, Nirmala's father would not have asked for police protection this year."

Shakti said, "Yes, my father knows the district administrator well. You know that his bungalow is nearby. His family keeps coming to Kashtaharni Ghat for pujas. Even I have gone there to perform rituals at times. I think it is best that we take his help. But I am not sure to what extent he would share details with us."

"I think that is not a good idea. Policemen are anyway suspicious in nature. We would not be able to give any strong reason for enquiring. But I think that if I go to my father's office, I might get more information."

❀ ❀ ❀

Chapter 20

The Truth Behind Previous Year's Incident

Rakesh belonged to a family of lawyers. His father, grandfather and great grandfather, all had been prominent lawyers in the local court. His father was expected to be promoted to judge in next few months. In fact, Rakesh's father was quite disappointed when he learned that Rakesh was not pursuing law for his career.

The next day, Rakesh went to his father's office inside the court premises.

"How are you, Ramu," he asked the peon sitting outside his father's office.

"I am fine sir! Looks like the sun has risen from the other side today! Or have you lost your way?" quipped the peon. He had been on duty since more than two decades. He was very close to Rakesh's family and often used to visit their home. He had developed an avid interest in the ongoing cases. Although he did not go through any files, he himself was a repository of information, mostly heard from others.

He also had a sharp memory. If he did not know about a case, then that case itself had to be insignificant.

"Father says that I need to be more serious now with my career. So I thought of coming here and checking how exciting this work can be!" His father had left for a meeting with a client and was not expected back for another two hours. "Come! Let us have some tea under that banyan tree. You can tell me more in the pleasant sun in this winter."

"What do you find exciting here, Ramu dada?"

"Dear, nothing can be more exciting than this place! Just keep coming here for few days. It can be more much more exciting than the Bond movies that kids of your age watch." He was referring to James Bond movies that he had heard Rakesh talking about few times.

"Really? So, tell me. Which is the most exciting case you have seen in your entire life here?"

"Rakesh baba, I can quote you several. But the best is the one in which your father almost stole away an old man from his death bed."

Rakesh remembered. An old man had been charged of killing his son. All circumstantial evidences were against him. He had not even hired any lawyer to fight his case. When Rakesh's father saw the old man, he sensed as if the old man had surrendered to his fate. He then took the old man in confidence and became his lawyer without charging any fees. He worked almost day and night for next few days and uncovered that although the son had abandoned the old man few years back, the son had been killed by his uncle over a land dispute. The vile uncle had planted proof in such a way that it pointed towards the old man. After almost three months of relentless work, Rakesh's father had been able to crack the case. It was well covered by the local newspapers and brought a lot of goodwill for him.

"I remember, Ramu dada. The sense of satisfaction that dad got from the case was much more than the accolades. That was one of the rare cases that I saw him getting emotionally attached with."

"Yes, your father was in touch with the old man till the time he was alive."

There was a long pause. It appeared that both were remembering those details in the solitude of their minds. After a while, Rakesh spoke, "Ramu dada, I went to Sita Kund few days back. You know the annual fare that happens there. One of my friends was going there to assist in the arrangements. I had accompanied him. It was strange to see that this time, there were policemen keeping guard there. I was talking to some people there. They mentioned that there was a law and order problem last year." He paused there to see if Ramu would add more to the conversation without prodding. That would not raise any unnecessary suspicion.

Ramu took the bait, "Yes, there was a big problem last year. The priest's daughter had been abducted. But she returned home safely that evening. I think the matter closed there." Ramu had suddenly become serious. "Leave that. How are your studies going on? What do you plan to do next?"

Rakesh sensed that Ramu did not want to talk about the issue. He hugged him tightly and whispered, "Dada, I think I like the girl! Please do not speak about it to anyone. That is the reason why I want to know more."

"Ah, so that is why you have come here today! You could just ask the girl directly!" Ramu said with a smile. He knew that this is not a subject that Rakesh would have discussed with anyone else in his family. Ramu had known Rakesh since his childhood. He loved Rakesh liked his own child. But his smile vanished the next moment. "You are young. You can find so many girls. What is it that you saw in her? I do not think that you should pursue this matter." He had grown worried.

Rakesh was perturbed now. "But what is wrong in liking Nirmala?" He was desperate to know more. "Ramu dada, Please tell me all that you know. I am very curious. Even if you do not, you know that I will find about her from somewhere or the other. I have not mentioned it to anyone. I thought that you could help me in knowing the correct version of the incident."

Ramu sighed. He looked at the clock at the top of the court. Rakesh's father would still take another hour to be back. "Listen, you could land up in trouble with her. I will tell you what I know. But I must caution you to be very careful. What is her name…ah…Nirmala! Last year, Vikram's gang had kidnapped her from the temple. Vikram is a dreaded goon. He has a very big gang at Bardah village. You know the typical Robin Hood type of goons. He is a big smuggler of arms but splurges a small part of the booty with the village inhabitants. The whole village treats him like a Demi-God. It is said that he had developed a liking for her. A total of nine heavily armed men had gone to the temple to abduct her last year. Nirmala also put up a brave fight. But then, she was hurt and they took her in their jeep. There were so many people there. But no one came to help her. Her father kept pleading but the men would not listen. But Nirmala was back by the evening. That jeep was found charred along with three men of Vikram's gang. One of the three was Vikram's young brother. There was a fourth body which was unidentified. The police found a bottle of alcohol nearby and the jeep had rammed itself against a boulder. They concluded that the fourth man was drunk. He was walking on the middle of the unpaved road. The jeep swerved to save him and rammed onto the boulder. The impact made a hole in the fuel tank and it ignited, burning all four men to death. Somehow, Nirmala escaped unscathed from there and returned home. There was a big outcry over the incident. Few prominent people had visited the police chief after that. There have already been several cases pending against Vikram in various courts. The police then raided Bardah and a few other hide outs just a month later. Vikram escaped and has been underground since then."

Rakesh had read the same version from the newspaper articles. He wanted to know more. Who exactly was this Vikram? How dangerous was he? Was he a threat now also? Was Nirmala safe? His mind was full of questions.

"Dada. It has been one year since the incident. In the whole period, has Vikram or his men ever come back to threaten Nirmala again?"

"No. But there are stories going around that he has returned just a few days back. That is the reason why Sita Kund had asked for police protection this time. Most people believe that Vikram would seek revenge."

Rakesh was angry, "What revenge? It was his men who had kidnapped Nirmala? And they died on their own? Revenge for what?"

"Rakesh baba, that is why I asked you to keep away. But I know that once you set your mind on anything, it would not be easy for you to let go. What I told you was the official version. That is what most people are aware of. But one of the policemen who went to investigate is a very good friend of mine. He confided in me that it was not the fire that had killed all those four men. The fourth man, whose identity is not clear, died in the fire. That is sure. But the three gang members including Vikram's younger brother had most probably died even before the fire."

Rakesh was confused. "If the fire did not kill them, then who did?" He was not ready for the answer that came.

After a long pause, Ramu looked around if there was anyone near enough to hear them and said in a hushed tone, "Nirmala."

Rakesh could not believe his ears. She looked so lean and feeble. How could it be her? He was anxious to know more.

"Even before they kidnapped Nirmala, she had fought the nine men all alone at the temple. But she was hit from behind by the butt of a rifle. Else, they would not have been able to kidnap her."

Rakesh was completely lost. Nirmala fought nine men alone? Did he hear it right? As many as nine hardened criminals would not have been able to kidnap her if she was not hit from behind? Rakesh was in complete disbelief.

Ramu continued, "The postmortem report was changed under police pressure by the local doctor. He was also transferred only days later to some other city altogether overnight. No one knows where he went. I was told that all three gang men had died of serious internal injuries."

"Yeah, the jeep had tumbled right! So it is likely that they would have been hurt badly. What is wrong with that?"

"No. They had injuries that bore the likelihood of a precise martial art attack. In fact, after few bottles of alcohol, my friend told me that he believed it had to be Nirmala and no one else. But to save Nirmala, the police team had floated the theory that most know about. It is also said that although Vikram had gone hiding during the raids, he has been enquiring about the incident. Although, he might not know the exact truth, he holds Nirmala responsible for the death of his younger brother. You know how things are with these criminals. They need a purpose to keep alive and that purpose has to be evil!"

Rakesh was speechless. He could still not reconcile the picture of the shy girl whom he had met few months back at Ram Kund with the warrior like image that Ramu was presenting in front of him now.

Suddenly he saw his father alighting from his motorcycle. He quickly whispered to Ramu, "Dada, not a word please with my father!"

"Sure, but you need to promise me that you will share anything that happens in this case with me on a regular basis. I expect to see you more often here." His love for Rakesh made him command that kind of promise. Rakesh nodded in affirmative.

❁ ❁ ❁

Chapter 21
Danger Comes Closer

"Rakesh, can you fetch me the newspaper?" asked Rakesh's father. Rakesh picked up the newspaper from outside the door. He nonchalantly handed him the newspaper. His father usually took the main paper and left the local edition for reading later. It was important to know the bigger things going on at more important places. Local stuff could wait for his attention. Anyway, time moved slowly here. He kept the local section on the table. His mother brought tea. As she was setting the cup down, it slipped a bit and spilled some tea on the table. She immediately took out a paper from the local section of the newspaper to wipe out. Rakesh came forward to help. As he bent to remove other things from the table, his eyes fell on an article in the local edition. The title said, "Doctor Sanjay murdered: Bardah man suspect." His heartbeat started pacing.

He carefully took that section and ran to the place where the phone lay. He called up his father's office. "Hello, lawyer Prasad's office," said Ramu from the other side.

"Dada, it is me."

Ramu could sense urgency in his voice. "What happened? Is everything alright?"

"Did you see the local newspaper today?"

"I am yet to complete the cleaning, Rakesh baba. Newspaper comes only after that."

"Please read the local section, page three immediately. Is it the same guy?"

Ramu could not understand anything. He kept the receiver on the table without disconnecting the phone and turned to the third page in the local section. His hands were shaking, "Baba, come here as soon as you get time. And stay away from the girl!"

Rakesh could almost hear his heartbeat. His mother called, "Go and have your bath. I am cooking radish stuffed paratha today." But Rakesh wasn't hearing anything anymore. He stepped out of his house. He took his scooter and went out.

"Shakti, Shakti, come out!" he almost shouted outside Shakti's house. Shakti also came out in a hurry.

"What happened? Is everything alright?"

"Come immediately with me!"

Shakti rode on the back seat. "What has happened? Tell me! Is everything alright at home?" He asked at the top of his voice. But Rakesh was not listening, partly due to the wind blowing past his ears and more importantly because of the article that he had read.

"What is the meaning of this Ramu dada?" asked Rakesh. Ramu looked worried. He looked at Shakti. Rakesh said, "Oh come on dada! You know that Shakti and I are childhood friends. There is hardly any secret between us. Now please tell us what you make of this news."

Shakti was lost as to what were they talking about.

"The whole of Bardah is indebted to Vikram. Although I hope it is not true, but if anyone from Bardah is involved, it cannot be without the knowledge of Vikram, which means that he has been successful at least in finding out the doctor."

The mention of Vikram's name sent chills down Shakti's spine. He had sensed that Rakesh had been enquiring about Nirmala. But the mention of the dreaded goon gave him a bad feeling. When Ramu told him the whole story again, Shakti got even more scared.

"Rakesh, I fully agree with Ramu dada that we should keep out of this. It is getting darker and darker. We are very simple people. We cannot take on such hardcore criminals. Had it been some small-time miscreant, I would not have doubted that without anyone's help also, we could handle the situation. But this is a completely different and much more dangerous situation. If you…". Even before he could complete his sentence, Rakesh pulled him to the scooter. "Come with me. Thank you, Ramu dada."

Without waiting for a reply from Ramu, he drove off. He parked the scooter near the Kashtaharni Ghat. He held Shakti's hand and went to a secluded place on the bank of the river Ganges. "Shakti, I had told you that I liked Nirmala. I was wrong. I think I have fallen in love with her. You know, from the time I bumped into her during our exploration last year, I have never been able to take my minds off her. I met her just a few days back along with you after a long time. But I feel as if she was always with me since we bumped at Ram Kund."

"Please try to understand, Rakesh." But Rakesh was not listening. He was staring some distance across the river.

"Come what may, I will try to save her from these men. I know its going to be dangerous. But I guess that is my fate now." His face was full of anger. His body was stiff. His chest had come out. Shakti knew his friend well. Rakesh never gave up if he set his eyes on something. He may win or lose, but he would not give up unless he was satisfied that he had given his efforts adequately. He knew that it was useless to say anything to him now. He had made his decision.

"So what is your fate, is ours too!" said Shakti trying hard to bring a smile on his face.

"No, Shakti, I know it is dangerous. We are best friends. But from here, the journey sounds very difficult. I would rather not put you in danger."

"You selfish piece of shit!" shouted Shakti. "When I saw the opportunity of the adventure at Mir Qasim's tunnel, I shared it with both you and Binod. Now that an exciting life awaits you, you are ditching us?"

Rakesh understood the pun and let out a faint laugh. All three of them- Binod, Rakesh and Shakti had been friends since childhood. They had studied in the same primary and secondary schools. They were together even in college. But when it came to post graduation, Binod, the sharpest of the three, secured admission into one of the most reputed institutes in the country. It was only then that they had separated. Binod was now in his final year and would be returning home in another two months.

❁ ❁ ❁

Chapter 22
Face to Face with Nirmala

The next day, Rakesh and Shakti went to Sita Kund together. It was the last day of the annual fare. They had not gone as volunteers but they wanted to speak to Nirmala directly. Rakesh parked his scooter some distance away from the temple. Rakesh wanted to talk to the volunteers and escape the long queue. But Shakti insisted to follow rules and not create any commotion. There were women and children waiting to enter the temple. It took them almost half an hour to enter the temple. This was perhaps one of the longest wait that Rakesh had experienced ever. As they entered, Shakti said, "Why don't you go and find Nirmala? In the meantime, I will go and offer my prayers inside the temple. After all, we need lots of blessings."

Rakesh could not find Nirmala or her father anywhere. He went near the room inside the temple premises. He saw from the distance that they were sitting inside with a policeman. This was different from the skull cap wearing policemen deployed for the annual fare. This one had a hard cap which appeared more impressive. It appeared that he was some senior officer. He wanted to hear what was being talked about. He slipped near the window and grabbed the broom that was lying near the window so that one would think that he was doing some work there and not eavesdropping.

"Pandit ji, we believe that the doctor was murdered on the orders of Vikram. We are not sure if he has learnt the truth. But it is quite possible. We will keep the pressure on him. But he has lots of sympathizers not only at Bardah but across several other places as well. Honestly, our local police are no match for the strength that he has. Over the years, few corrupt officers have allowed him to grow. And the demon that he has grown into is much bigger than the force that we have here. People believe that he had fled last time because of the older case that we had started investigation. But I am now told that he was onto something else which had kept him occupied. It appears that he has now completed that task."

Nirmala didn't say anything. Her father said, "We are grateful that you came here and apprised us of the situation. We understand the gravity of the situation. But we are poor people. Most of my relatives have already departed to the other world. Very few are alive. They all stay around this place only. I do not want anything bad to happen to my child. But I am unable to think of a place where I can send her safely. More importantly, we still do not understand what exactly he wants from Nirmala! She is such a good soul. She has never harmed anyone. Why would anyone be after her?"

"Pandit ji, I do not have any answer to this question. I am also not able to fathom a solid reason." After a brief pause, he added very hesitatingly, "I am not sure. But it could just be that he saw Nirmala somewhere and is… smitten. You know how these criminals are. I do not know what to say."

Nirmala finally spoke for the first time so far, "Inspector, thank you very much for all your help so far. It has been of great help in avoiding any untoward incident this year. Is it possible for you to tell us more about Vikram? If you can tell us exactly the things that you know, even if it is unconfirmed, it would help us greatly in keeping ourselves safe."

Rakesh wanted to move closer to hear. In his anxiety, he did not notice the pot which was kept nearby. His broom touched the pot. The inspector came out running to check. But Rakesh had managed to slip into the crowd nearby. Nirmala had also come near the window and spotted someone slipping away. She looked further as the person vanished into the crowd. Had she seen him somewhere?

"No one knows much about him. It appears that he was orphaned at an early age. He was adopted by the Thakur family at Bardah. This is a family of landlords. By the virtue of money and power, they have been oppressing the poor and the needy since ages. They often used to lend money at high rates to poor farmers and then grab their lands when they were not able to pay their outstanding debt. And over time, they started employing goons for debt recovery or for land grabbing. Slowly but steadily, the size of the gang increased. Completely unchecked, they soon slipped away into the business of manufacturing illegal arms and smuggling. Vikram, probably hardened through a troubled childhood, took the crime to altogether different level. He has now become the face of the family. He has expanded his business to not only nearby states but also to nearby countries like

Bangladesh, Nepal and Myanmar. He is known to be very ruthless. Several cases have been filed against him. But the supply of money, strong connections with people across political, judicial and enforcement agencies have ensured that nothing has happened to him."

"But he has strong support at Bardah. He is more cunning than the Thakur who adopted him. Since he took charge, he has been helping his villagers generously and they in turn provide him with much required cover. He can be spotted in the village. But whenever we reach there, he vanishes into thin air, all with the help of the village folks."

Nirmala interrupted, "Inspector, if he wanted to see me so much that he sent a group of nine men including his brother to fetch me, what I am unable to understand is why did he not make any attempt for almost another year? When you raided his hideouts, he had gone into hiding. But for so long? What do you think could be the reason?"

"We believe that he did not go into hiding because of our raids. My sense is that there was some more important work which could not be avoided. We are also not sure about it. But it appears that the mission is over now and our sources have spotted him in nearby villages. That's why I thought of warning you myself. If you want, I can put two policemen here on some pretext or the other. But honestly, they would not be any match if his men come."

Nirmala said, "Thank you very much, sir. It is very kind of you. But as you said, it might not be effective."

The inspector said, "I think you should make a representation to the Chief Minister directly. Maybe he can offer some help."

Nirmala's father said standing up, "Thank you very much sir. Let me think over it. We will surely make a representation to him. Now, we must go back and tend to the devotees. It is the last day and many of the volunteers have also become tired now."

As Nirmala came out of the room, she could spot Rakesh in the crowd. He was standing in the crowd, but his eyes were still locked towards the room. He turned away quickly when he realized that the meeting with the inspector was over.

"You missed most of it," said Nirmala as she stood next to Rakesh. Rakesh was completely taken aback. He did not even know when and how did she come near him.

"I… I…", he was too lost. But then he saw that Nirmala wasn't angry and in fact she smiled as he felt embarrassed that he was caught and fumbled for words. "I am sorry. I should not have heard."

"Do you want to have some tea?"

❁ ❁ ❁

Chapter 23

A do-or-die Moment

Rakesh was feeling uncomfortable. After all, this was the moment he had been waiting for since long time. And now that he was with her, he was not sure how and what to talk.

Nirmala said, “That inspector was just warning us. I am sure you would have heard about me. I am not that worried about myself, but I just do not want others getting hurt because of me.”

Rakesh finally opened his mouth, “I know. You are very brave. What will you do now?”

“Do you know that story? When lion comes in front of the goat, ‘doing’ is the prerogative of the lion!”

Both let out a small laugh. There was a brief pause. Nirmala said, “I don’t know why Vikram wants to meet me. It is killing me to just wait here for him to come. Maybe I should just go and seek him out. It is so embarrassing to be the cause of pain to so many people. My father has been under so much stress since last year. And the devotees had to go through all this unnecessary security this year. I saw so many women and kids waiting in the sun. They had to wait just because of me."

Rakesh saw that her fists were clenched. Her eyes had become watery. She was feeling sad and was also angry. He did not know what to say or do. They were both looking far away into the horizon. His eyes had also become misty.

Suddenly there was a lot of commotion at the entrance. Shakti was running towards them. "Run away Nirmala! Looks like Vikram's gang has come. Run, run!"

Shakti's eyes were filled with fear. But Rakesh's eyes were filled with fire. Nirmala's eyes were calm like still water. She heaved a sigh. She said in a feeble tone, "Running will not help friends."

Rakesh was surprised how Nirmala had maintained a cold demeanor despite the danger that lay ahead. They could hear few gun shots in the air. And then the commotion itself was so much that even if bullets were fired, no one could hear it. The crowd dispersed immediately. Within no time, the temple had become empty. The police guards at the gate had already surrendered their rifles. Who would fight such dreaded criminals?

Vikram caught hold of one of the men on the way. He was asking something. He twisted his hand as he did not receive any answer. He then caught hold of one of the priests. "Where is Nirmala?" The priest was too nervous to say anything. His body was shaking. He lifted his hand to point towards the room outside which Nirmala, Rakesh and Shakti were standing.

Vikram was almost 6'3 tall, slightly taller than Rakesh. His shoulders were broad. His cheek bones were protruding.

The muscles around his neck almost formed a triangle. His wide chest was almost oozing out of his t-shirt. He had a big frame. He had two accomplishes, one on each side. Both were holding some modern looking machine guns. Vikram was not carrying anything.

Rakesh gauged that Vikram would definitely weigh more than a hundred kilograms. Rakesh was fearful of what might happen next. Shakti took a few steps back. Nirmala had not moved. Rakesh was on her side. As the three goons came nearer, Rakesh came in front of Nirmala. He was full of anger. He spotted an iron rod kept near the window. He knew that he was no match for a person like Vikram, but how could he let anything happen to Nirmala?

In a very heavy but calm tone, about four feet away, Vikram said, “Move aside. I only want her.” His accomplices were standing a step behind, looking around and keeping an eye on the surroundings.

“Why are you after her? What has she done? Leave her alone!” Rakesh’s eyes were continuously switching between Vikram and the iron rod.

Nirmala’s father had also come nearer by that time. With folded hands and a bent frame, he was almost begging, “We are simple people. We spend most of our time in the temple praying to God. What have we done to you? Why do you want to harm her?” Tears were trickling down his eyes.

One of the two goons caught hold of Nirmala’s father.

Nirmala, who had not said a word yet, shouted standing behind Rakesh, “Leave my father alone!”

Even before Rakesh could think of what to do, he felt a hand on his right shoulder from behind. Nirmala had put her left hand on his right shoulder and taking the support, she had flown into the air towards Vikram. Even before Vikram could see, she bent her right knee and hit hard on Vikram's temple. She knew that a hit like that could knock senses out of a strong man, if not make him unconscious. She was surprised to see that although Vikram fell down, he was far from being hurt grievously. He quickly jumped back on his feet.

Rakesh realized that the line had been crossed; it was a do-or-die situation. He lunged towards the iron rod. He was also an athlete of strong built. Vikram was back on his feet lurking towards Nirmala. He swerved the iron rod onto Vikram. Vikram tried to duck. The rod hit his accomplice and the gun fell from his hand. He writhed in pain as the rod hit him hard on his ribs. He immediately sat down clutching his ribs. The other accomplish let go of Nirmala's father and dashed towards Rakesh. Vikram was back on his feet and lunged towards Nirmala. She tried to punch him hard but he ducked it easily. She then stepped on the side, shuffled her legs and tried to hit him with a side kick. But Vikram was careful this time and ducked that too.

Shakti shouted for help but no one was coming forward. He moved towards one of the goons. But he had never been in a fight ever before, not even as a kid. His only skirmishes had been verbal and that too, he only stood firm when it came to religious discussions. Rest all, he would give up soon.

The goon hit him hard with the gun. The gun hit him hard on his back. Shakti let out a loud cry and fell down.

Rakesh could see the blood on Shakti's back. He hit that man on his legs with the rod. The man fell down.

In the meantime, as Nirmala was preparing to hit Vikram again, he quickly turned around and hit Nirmala hard on her abdomen. Nirmala could not duck and was hit hard. She clutched her stomach. But the next moment, she moved her leg to create a vertical arch and tried to hit him on his chest. But Vikram swiftly moved aside and punched her on her face. Nirmala's lips were cut. She was bleeding. Her father kept shouting for help. But no one was coming forward. The old man did not know what to do. Rakesh shouted, "Vikram, I will kill you!" He came near and aimed to hit him with the rod on his head. Vikram raised his hands and caught the rod with his hands. The attack was hard, but Vikram was able to avoid it hitting him on his head. Realizing that the attack had gone to waste, Rakesh came closer to hit him on his face. Vikram had dropped the rod. He moved aside and punched Rakesh hard on his chest. Rakesh was unable to take the punch. He fell down immediately.

Nirmala was furious. She turned around and launched a roundhouse kick on Vikram. Her foot landed on Vikram's head. But he was still standing firmly. He moved beside Nirmala swiftly and caught hold of her neck. He quickly took out a white handkerchief and put it to her nose. The sweet smelling chloroform had again knocked her down completely. Vikram's associates had partly recovered by this time. Vikram carried Nirmala on his back. Rakesh tried to stand up. He picked up the rod and ran towards Vikram. But one of the goons hit him hard and the other took a similar handkerchief and knocked him unconscious too.

Shakti was still lying down, blood coming out of his back. Nirmala's father sat on the ground crying for help. The two goons fired few gun shots in the air to discourage anyone who might want to obstruct their way. Vikram and his goons carried Nirmala to the jeep. The policemen had left long back along with the inspector.

❁ ❁ ❁

Chapter 24
Rakesh Goes to Bardah

Rakesh opened his eyes and found himself in his home the next morning. His body ached from yesterday's fight. His head was still heavy from the after effects of the high dose of chloroform. He suddenly started running out of his house. His mother shouted at him, "Where are you going?" He found his father standing at the door. His face showed that he was very angry.

"What is this all about? You could be dead yesterday if the police had not ringed me up!"

"Father, I will explain this later, I need to go now urgently." He muttered in a low voice.

"What do you think you are doing? I have been told everything about this incident. You got involved just because you were there yesterday. Just forget about it and do not try to meddle in unnecessary things!" His father shouted at the top of his voice.

Rakesh knew that it was useless to argue at this point of time. But he loved Nirmala. He had seen her being carried away. Who will save her? What did Vikram want from her?

His heart was bleeding and his head was spinning with so many questions.

His father caught hold of his hand and took him inside the hall. His mother also came along. She was crying. His father was calmer now. He made him sit on the sofa.

"Listen Rakesh! Vikram is a very dreaded criminal. I know about him very well. He is someone that even the police here can't handle. He has strong connections with politicians also, not only in Munger but across neighboring states as well. He has spread his tentacles across neighboring countries as well. I am not sure why has he taken Nirmala. But you need to stay away from this. He may even forgive you for meddling in his affairs yesterday. But if you try to get involved now, he will never forgive us. We can only fight legal cases. We cannot fight with guns. Vikram is not alone. He has a very big gang of loyal criminals. You will not even know whom to fight. He can knock us off very easily. Police will also not be able to do much."

Rakesh did not say anything. He could still hear voices from yesterday. He felt as if Nirmala was crying for help. He muttered in a soft voice, "Father, you have fought so hard all these years to deliver justice to people. Nirmala is such a simple girl. Instead of us trying to help her, you are also discouraging me from helping her. God knows what that monster will do to her if we do not intervene!" He said, almost pleading.

"Both of those things are different, Rakesh. Arguing in a court is different. We are civilized people. How can we fight such criminals? If it were small criminals, we could still manage. We could take the help of the state machinery! But Vikram is above the law in this region! Even if we want, we would not be able to do anything. We will end up killing ourselves only!"

His mother then took him to his room and sat beside him. She brought him breakfast. While he was eating, he heard the servant shouting, "Prasad sir, Prasad sir." They ran to the hall.

Rakesh's father Prasad was speaking on the phone. He was sweating. Prasad put the phone down and hurried outside. "I am going to the court. It seems that someone has beaten Ramu badly. Rakesh, you stay inside the house. Don't go anywhere."

He rushed to his motorcycle and was gone the next moment. Rakesh's mother went inside. But the hall was empty. Rakesh was nowhere to be found. She searched around, but Rakesh had already left. The servant ran to her with a piece of paper which read "Mother, I am going to Bardah. Please do not worry about me. I will be back by the evening."

Chapter 25
Fleeing Away from Bardah

Bardah was a small village with hardly few thousand people living there. People were largely engaged in farming. Few had become local merchants. During the British rule, the first arms factory was opened at Munger. With time, the factory was closed down. However, lack of opportunities easily attracted the youth towards the art which still flourished in few old hands. Youth of Bardah, unable to find a suitable opportunity, were largely engaged in manufacturing illegal arms. There was a local school and a small hospital. It was almost 10am and most shops were just opening up. There was a small Hanuman temple.

Rakesh had left his scooter outside the village. He quickly covered his face with a shawl. He was still in his sleepers. He desperately wanted to go to Vikram's house as early as possible. But he had no idea as to where did he live. He could see the Hanuman temple nearby. It did not seem crowded. He could hear the bells of the temple ringing at intervals. As he approached nearer, he sat on the steps leading to the temple and started pretending like a beggar.

He started asking for alms sitting there. There were two more beggars sitting beside him. As an old lady came down from the temple, he said, "Mother, please give me some money. I have not eaten anything since yesterday." He wanted to start a conversation which he could direct towards finding Vikram's location.

"I have not seen you here earlier. Are you new to this place?"

"Yes, I am a poor person. I have not been keeping well. I was just roaming around and landed up here. I will bless your kids. Please give me some money."

"Our kids already have the blessing of Vikram dada. And God has sent him to take care of us." She handed him few coins.

"I have heard so much about him. Where can I meet him? I want to beg him to help me as well. I have not been keeping well and will die otherwise in this cold weather."

"Just keep going straight. There is a big farmhouse at the end there. Ask any of the men there to take you inside." She pointed to a far off place.

Rakesh thanked her and pretending to limp, he carried off in that direction. His heart was beating fast. What if he got caught inside? No one would even know if he is killed. What if Nirmala was not there? Then his sacrifice would also go waste. But was there any other way? If he had to help Nirmala, then he had to risk his life.

He had his head covered in the shawl. Anyway, only two of Vikram's goons had seen him. No one would recognize him. But people would be wary of any stranger in the village. It was a small village and people knew everything about each other. He moved cautiously.

The semi-concrete road with numerous potholes had only few people roaming around. He saw the big farmhouse in a distance. The entrance had boundary walls which were almost four feet high. He could see what lay inside. There was a big garden just inside the boundary wall. He wanted to do a full recce before entering the house. He went on the side to take a full round of the farmhouse. He saw that there was a two storied house at the center. The house was really large. There were 5-6 gardeners working in the garden around the house. Two jeeps were parked inside the boundary. A brand new motorcycle was also parked inside. There was a small stable at the back. Although he could not see inside, he could hear the sound of few horses. On the top of the house, he could see a few men roaming around. They were not armed. But their body built suggested that they were no ordinary villagers. But almost on all sides, he felt as if one or more person always kept guard. Probably they had arms hidden somewhere nearby.

As he was thinking of how to enter without getting caught, he saw a shining sedan sliding towards the main gate of the farmhouse. It was quickly followed by two SUVs. All had dark windows. The road itself was not good. So they were coming slowly. Some villagers had started following them on foot, probably to check if these were friends or foes of their God, Vikram dada.

The sedan stopped at the gate. The back window of the last SUV rolled down and suddenly, someone fired a few rounds of bullets into the air. Few people from the crowd, mainly women and children dispersed but the men came back with long sticks. By that time, the last SUV had turned itself facing the crowd. Few musclemen came out of it with very sophisticated looking guns. One of the men shouted, "Do not come near us. We will shoot you down." The voice was ferocious. One man had stepped out of the sedan. The main gate was made of iron grill. There was a large lock dangling from inside. He pulled out his pistol and broke open the door as he fired onto it. He went inside the sedan and the sedan entered the farmhouse. The last SUV kept guard at the gate facing the crowd while the other one went inside after the sedan. As they stopped, a group of more than ten men came outside the door of the house with various kinds of firearms.

Rakesh had seen so many firearms in the movies only. He was sweating profusely. He realized that the whole thing was going on just at the front of the farmhouse. He quickly slipped from the back side. The boundary was small. He quickly jumped over the wall and came inside. By that time, there was a lot of commotion outside the farmhouse. Hordes of men with sticks had come in front of the SUV. They sensed that there was some danger to Vikram. Few men tried to step forward and hit the six men from the SUV. The men from the SUV appeared ruthless. One of them opened fire. It was aimed low. Bullets hit two men below their knees. Rest became alert. The crowd stepped back. Someone from the crowd hurled a stone towards them. It hit one of the men. But he quickly fired few bullets into the crowd, again at low level. Two more men got hurt below their knees. The crowd moved further back. There were blood spots at few places. The men from the SUV shouted, "Stay away from this. We do not want to hurt you. But if you insist on interfering, then we do not mind killing you. We are heavily armed. Go to your homes."

At the entrance, there were tens of Vikram's people acting as guards, their guns pointing towards the intruders. Suddenly, three men stepped out of the sedan. One of them shouted, "Do not do anything foolish. We want to talk to Vikram. We know he is here." As he heard one of them unlocking his firearm, he suddenly took out his pistol and fired at that person. The man fell on the ground. The bullet had lodged deep inside his stomach. He had only few hours in this world. "Ask Vikram to come out. Else, we will kill all of you."

Vikram came out, without anything in his hands. It appeared that he knew the men and was already expecting them. He said coolly, "Let us talk inside. Leave them here."

The three men went inside the house. Six more men from the other SUV inside the boundary were standing at the door facing the gang. They were heavily armed and appeared much stronger than Vikram's men.

Amid all this melee, Rakesh saw that there was a balcony besides which was a drainage pipe. He quickly scaled it and landed on the balcony. He took out the knife that he had tied to his arm. A knife would not be any match to the kind of firearms that he had seen. But it could be very helpful in a close encounter. He peeped inside the French wooden window. There was no one inside. Probably all had gone to the front of the house. But where was Nirmala? He had to find her out quickly! He pushed the wooden window inside. There was a low screeching sound as he opened the window. He waited for a moment to check if someone had noticed the sound. When he was sure that no one was there, he entered the room. There was another room on the opposite side. But he heard footsteps. He carefully hid himself behind the door of the room. He had never heard his heartbeat so loud. Could others hear it? He wondered! He was praying all this while.

"Vikram. You have disappointed us." Vikram, accosted by the three men, was coming up. What if they came inside this room? Was it the last day of his life?

Luckily, he heard them going to the opposite room. Rakesh wanted to hear what they were saying. The door behind which he was hiding had a small crack. He could not hear much but he was able to see what was going on inside the room on the opposite side. He saw that Vikram was sitting on the bed while one of the three men was sitting in front of him. The other two were standing on either side with their firearms. The men were facing the door, probably so that they could keep a watch on any possible danger coming up. Rakesh could see them clearly. The man sitting on the chair had a beard and his face was almost covered behind a large and dark sunglass. When the man took off his sunglasses, Rakesh realized that it was not an Indian but a foreigner. One of the two men standing also appeared to be a foreigner.

The man seemed furious at Vikram. His hands were waving wildly when he was talking. Suddenly, he stood up and shouted something in a foreign language. Vikram did not stand up. He just kept quiet. His head was hanging down. He just nodded in affirmative. Then he stood up and the three men started coming out of the room. At the door, the man turned around to face Vikram and said, "This is the last warning. You need to complete the task that you had promised. Else, we all will die." These jokers of yours will not be able to save you.

Suddenly, they heard gun shots from the ground floor where Vikram's men and the intruders were facing each other. Vikram and the men ran down to see what was happening. Rakesh took this opportunity to go inside the room on the opposite side. To his utter surprise, he found Nirmala tied to a chair. Her eyes were open and a cloth was stuck inside her mouth. He quickly took out his knife and cut the rope. She took out the cloth from her mouth. She did not say anything but her eyes had become moist as she stared at Rakesh. Rakesh quickly dragged her to the room from where he had entered the house. He quickly looked down. There was no one there. Everyone was engrossed in the new problem that had arisen at the front of the house. To hell with them, he thought.

He first let Nirmala slide down the drain pipe. He knew that there was hardly any time left. He jumped without caring to slide down the drain pipe. There was a lot of noise coming from the front and he was sure that the sound he made while landing on the ground had gone unnoticed. He quickly got up.

Without saying a word, they climbed the boundary wall. He took off his shawl and wrapped it around Nirmala. He took some soil from the ground and rubbed it on his face and shirt to make him look dirty and unrecognizable. They mingled in the crowd outside Vikram's farmhouse. Slowly, they slipped away. They soon reached the place where he had parked his scooter. They drove the scooter at maximum speed that was possible.

❀ ❀ ❀

Chapter 26

The Reason Behind Nirmala's Abduction

Back at Vikram's farmhouse, one of the men shouted, "Dada, she has escaped!"

Few hours ago, when he was upstairs with the foreigner, the brother of the man from Vikram's gang who had been shot, had not been able to stop himself and had started shouting at the intruders. While others were trying to control him, in the confusion, his gun fired a shot. That had led to one of the intruders also firing. By the time Vikram and the foreigner had come down, they found casualties at both sides. Three more of Vikram's men had died while one of the intruders had also been killed. There was blood everywhere.

Both Vikram and the foreigner calmed down their men. The foreigner then decided to leave the place. "Vikram, you must finish the work! I have my ears on you. Keep that in mind."

Vikram bowed and said "I understand. I will finish your work first." In front of the foreigner, he ordered one of his men, "Go and release that girl upstairs. Throw some water on her so that she awakens and ask her to leave immediately."

The intruders then left from Bardah immediately. They left back the dead man there itself.

"Dada, Nirmala has already escaped," said another of the men noticing that Vikram had not heard the earlier comment about her escape. Vikram let out a deep sigh. But then he had much more important things to do. Nirmala was important but not more than his life. He would come back later.

Rakesh kept running his scooter at full speed. Nirmala was sitting comfortably behind him. "You can drive slowly. We are already out of the village. There is no threat now." Was it the wind across his ears or was it out of fear of getting caught, Rakesh did not hear anything that Nirmala had said. She then put her hand gently on his shoulder.

Suddenly the scooter lost balance and both fell on the rough patch of the empty road. Rakesh fell far away, scratching his legs and hands against the unpaved road. Nirmala had managed to balance herself with her hands. As a result, she did not get hurt much except for few scratches on her hands. Her shawl had come off. She quickly got up and ran to Rakesh.

"Are you alright? You seem to be bruised all over!" Rakesh's clothes were torn at several places. He took the hand that Nirmala had let out for lifting him. But he completely forgot his pain. The left arm of her dress had been ripped off. He saw a familiar looking tattoo on Nirmala's bare arm. He had definitely seen the beautiful eye somewhere. But where?

"Hello! I am asking you something! Are you OK?"

But Rakesh was really lost, trying to figure out where exactly had he seen that eye.

"What are you staring at? This is my birth mark." Rakesh realized that he had been staring at her arm. He quickly lowered his eyes and said "Nothing." He looked around. There was no one following them.

The road was completely empty. They lifted the scooter and parked it on the side. There was a big rock there. Rakesh took out a water bottle from the scooter. They both took few sips.

"We are safe. Vikram and his gang will not come for me for at least another six months."

"What? How can you be so sure? What is it about six months? And who tore your dress?" Rakesh once again found his eyes on her bare arm which bore the birthmark so proudly. Glancing away, he also saw that she was wearing a steel bangle which mostly the Sikhs wore. He didn't fail to notice that the bangle also had a series of eyes made over it.

"When the foreigner and his gang came upstairs with Vikram, they thought that I was still unconscious. But I was just pretending. I heard them talk. It seems that the foreigner had given Vikram some work. The work has not yet been finished. Vikram left in between and came here. The foreigner warned Vikram to leave immediately and finish that work before doing anything else. They spoke in some foreign language at times. So, I could not understand what that unfinished task is. But Vikram was asking for at least nine months. The foreigner has given him only six months to complete the work. He further said that he had his moles inside Bardah. That is how he came to know when Vikram vanished into thin air without completing the work. He warned that he would keep strict vigil and if he sees him doing anything else, it would be dangerous for him and his men."

"God knows what these men keep doing! What I do not understand is how did you get involved?"

"I also don't know. I have not met any of these guys before. We have been living a very simple life. Vikram ripped off my dress." Nirmala pointed to the left arm where her cloth had been ripped off. "He was looking at my birth mark and was asking me about some crystal eye. He kept asking me several times. He said that since I have this birth mark, I must know about that crystal eye and its magic powers."

The last few words stunned Rakesh. Now he remembered where he had seen the tattoo like mark on Nirmala's left arm.

It was the biggest adventure of his life so far. It had just been last year when Binod, Shakti and he had discovered that crystal eye!

❁ ❁ ❁

Chapter 27
Flashback

Thousands of years ago…

The task was both physically and mentally challenging. The seven Ganas had to prepare for the greatest task of their lives, entrusted to them by none other than their master, the master of the whole universe, and the greatest of all Gods - Lord Shiva. Only one out of them was a female.

Under the direction of Nandi, they had to create a complex web of tunnels. It required phenomenal physical prowess. It had to be carried out in complete secrecy. They did not have much time at hand. They had been working tirelessly, but there was still so much to be done. The human form that they were about to take would have powers limited by the laws of mother earth.

Lord Shiva knew this. He took a stone from the ground and folded it in his hands tightly. The stone took the shape of an eye. He then opened his third eye. There was a blinding flash of light everywhere for a moment. All Ganas and Nandi closed their eyes. The light was gone in the next moment. When they opened their eyes, they could see that the stone in the hand of Shiva had turned into a crystal. There was a strong light emanating from it.

Shiva said, "Nandi, I cannot simply give powers to the Ganas when they become humans. I have put in special powers in this crystal. But they have to earn it. You need to tell them at an appropriate time."

The Ganas had been working for last few days and were completely exhausted. It was rare that their Lord ever asked anything of them. They did not want to disappoint him. They turned to Nandi. Nandi took out the crystal eye and thought, "We must find out how to unlock the powers that the Lord has given in the crystal eye."

On the advice of Nandi, they made a large Shivalinga there. They planted the crystal eye on it. Below the eye, they made a beautiful *chakra*. It had seven spokes, each in the form of a folded hand having an eye. They prayed night and day for the next three days, without moving from their place. Nandi knew that several devotees had sought blessings of Lord Shiva and other Gods and Goddesses by rigorous devotion and prayer. Lord Shiva had never disappointed anyone. How could he deny his blessings to the Ganas, that too when they were entrusted with a task so special by none other than himself!

And finally, there was a flash of light from the crystal eye. It lasted only for a fraction of a second. The Ganas had received immense strength from the Lord. They were now capable of the task that they had been chosen for.

Chapter 28

For love it is

Rakesh, Binod and Shakti had learnt about all this during their exploration of Mir Qasim's tunnel last year. It was a near death experience and revealed one of the most important unsaid mysteries of the oldest epic of all times, the Ramayana.

On the mention of the crystal eye by Nirmala, in a sudden flash, Rakesh's mind travelled back few months ago. It was a journey he could never forget. The three friends, Binod, Rakesh and Shakti had encountered an adventure of their lifetimes. How could they forget? They had become a part of the oldest epic that civilization had ever known!

Rakesh and his friends had learnt that the crystal eye was indeed magical. It could impart powers beyond human imagination. That is what helped the Ganas in playing such a critical role in the oldest epic in such a small-time window. But what was the extent of those powers? Or what was the process of actuating the crystal, the three friends had not been able to find out. They had also learnt that if someone with a bad motive tried to seek the powers of the crystal eye, then the crystal would destroy the person, just like the third eye of Shiva.

They had not tried to investigate more since they did not need any special powers anyway. All were doing well in life and had no ambition to rule the earth beyond what they could anyway achieve.

Ever since, they had promised to each other to keep it a secret. Let others find out if they could, but they would never share it with anyone. In fact, it was during those days only that Rakesh had first met Nirmala.

And in a sudden twist of things, it appeared that the story wasn't going to leave them yet.

Rakesh and Nirmala sat on the rock for a while. Nirmala said, "Let us go home now. Our parents would be worried."

Rakesh was still thinking about the crystal eye. He now realized why he found Nirmala's birth mark so strange. It was the same that he and his two friends had seen on the Shivalinga at the temple inside the Mir Qasim's tunnel.

Could it be just a mere coincidence? But then two coincidences - the birth mark on Nirmala's arm and the mention of the crystal eye by Vikram? It was hard for him to believe. It was becoming clearer that Vikram was not interested in Nirmala's beauty. He had ripped off her dress only to look at her birth mark. If Vikram had kidnapped Nirmala to know about the crystal eye, then did he also know the connection between the Ganas and the crystal eye? What more did he know about what they had found during their exploration last year? Could Nirmala be one of the descendants of the six Ganas? It was fairly possible since she had the same mark on her arm as made on the

Shivalinga inside the Mir Qasim's tunnel. But then how did Vikram come to know about it? Was he also a descendant? Did he also have the same mark on his arm? Where did he learn about the crystal eye? Were there more descendants of the six Ganas? Could there be others looking for the crystal eye?

"What are you thinking?" asked Nirmala.

"What exactly did Vikram ask you about the crystal eye?"

"Nothing specific. He just tore off the cloth on the arm and stared at my birth mark. Then he was shouting at me to tell him about some crystal eye. He was not ready to believe that I did not know about it. He warned me of consequences as well. But honestly, I do not know anything about it. He then again made me unconscious and thrust a cloth inside my mouth. Then I gained consciousness in some time and the rest you already know."

Rakesh said nothing and then they rode away.

Rakesh was thinking, "Six months is a long time. I would think of a way to make her safe. But more importantly, I have to find out the connection between her and the crystal eye. How did Vikram come to know about it anyway?"

He dropped her at Sita Kund. Nirmala said, "I do not know how to thank you. But why did you risk your life?" She was happy but wore a sad smile as she finished the last sentence. "I hope they do not know that you had come there. Else, you will also become a part of whatever this nonsense is all about." She was staring distant away.

"Do not worry. Take some rest. We will talk about it later. Looks like I have little choice anyway," Rakesh managed to smile.

Nirmala reached the temple to find that some goons had beaten the priests just after abducting her. It was perhaps meant to scare them away so that they would not put any bottleneck to whatever he was trying to achieve.

Back at Rakesh's place, his parents were happy that he had come home. But they were also very angry. His father, Prasad said, "Where had you gone? Do you know how worried we have been? What has happened to you? How have you been hurt?"

There was a volley of questions from his parents. His mother was still crying. He quickly went to his mother and said, "Do not worry mother. Look, I have returned safe and sound. I just fell down from the scooter and hurt myself."

He then recounted the whole story to his parents, all except the crystal eye. His father had gone through several cases of intimidation in the past since he became a lawyer. But Vikram was on a different level altogether. It was beyond his limits, in fact, it was beyond the capacity of anyone in the city to handle him.

Prasad said, "Look Vikram, do not get involved in this case. Vikram is just too dangerous. Several politicians and policemen are his stooges. We will not be able to fight him in any way." He continued further, "I had been to the court office today morning. Your uncle Ramu had been beaten up seriously. His leg has been broken. Doctor says it will remain in a cast for almost a month. I have a feeling as if it was the doing of Vikram's gang."

"I also got a call from Shakti's father few hours back. He got to know about Ramu. He also mentioned that when he was walking to the temple, someone hit him from behind on a motorcycle. He fell down. There were few of his friends around. The men on the motorcycle just rode away abusing him. He found it very strange. My sixth sense says that this could also be the handiwork of Vikram's gang."

"We are no match for such people. And anyway, I do not see a reason why you are getting involved in this case."

But his mother had sensed. Normally, women have stronger gut feeling. "Have you fallen in love with this girl? Why are you so quiet?"

"It is nothing like that."

"Go and take some rest first. Have some food. We will talk later," said his father sternly.

"Have you fallen in love with this girl?" His mother's question kept ringing in his ears for some time. How had his mother guessed it? If she had guessed it so far, then she would have also guessed his reply, he thought.

"Get up, Rakesh. It is almost dinner time now," called his mother. Rakesh did not realize how time had passed. The day had been very eventful. As they sat for dinner, no one spoke. There was a peculiar tension in the air. As usual, Rakesh had finished his dinner earlier than his parents. His mother said, "Go to your room and sleep. You are very tired."

After he had gone, Prasad said, "I also feel that he has developed a liking for this girl. Else, he would not have gone to this length."

Rakesh's mother, Vinita said, "I agree. But I am very worried now. I am not against him falling in love with a girl, no matter how she looks, what she does and where she comes from. I am not like our parents. But this is very complicated. We do not know how to fight such criminals. Even if we pull up all our connections, we may only keep Vikram at bay for a couple of months. If it had been only about him, then it would have been easier. But he controls a very large number of criminals. How can we ensure that none of them create problems?"

Prasad was in a very pensive mood. He did not say anything. He remembered that when he and Vinita were in love and had expressed their intention for marrying each other, they had faced lots of resistance from their parents. He was once beaten very badly. But then love is no less fierce. They had fought against all odds and gotten married. Prasad now saw Rakesh in a similar situation, even graver. He knew no matter what he said, he or Vinita would not be able to stop him.

❁ ❁ ❁

Chapter 29
Threat Worsens

Vinita, Rakesh's mother was sitting in the small garden in front of her house. Their house had a boundary wall about four feet high. It was mainly to assert the extent of their house rather than for safety. Suddenly, someone threw a big lizard which landed on her lap.

She screamed and went running to see who the miscreant was. She spotted two young chaps sneering at her. "What are you laughing at? Who threw it inside?" She was almost sure that it was none other than these two. She had never seen them in the locality.

"We have not thrown the lizard," laughed one of them.

"If you have not thrown, then how do you know that it was a lizard? How dare you do such things?" She had come out of the house and few passersby had started gathering there. By that time, Vinita's gardener, Bhim had also come out running.

The two youngsters had started hurtling abuses at Vinita. She was furious. She ran towards them, "Catch hold of these two guys. I will take them to the police."

Bhim came running along. But by the time he could come near, one of the youngsters took out a knife and stabbed Vinita in the back. Bhim caught one of them. But seeing Vinita lying in a pool of blood on the ground, his grip loosened. The two youngsters fled away.

Bhim shouted for Rakesh. Hearing the commotion, Rakesh came out of the house and was shocked to see his mother covered in blood. Bhim and Rakesh moved her inside the house and called up the ambulance. Rakesh took out some clothes and tried to tie it around the place where Vinita was bleeding from. His hands were also covered in blood. He was nervous and sweating. His father was away at the court. The ambulance took ten minutes to reach. It was one of the longest waits Rakesh had ever come across.

They reached the hospital in a while. Rakesh's father, Prasad rushed to the hospital directly. Vinita was in the ICU battling for her life. Doctors were busy going in and coming out. No one was telling them what was going on.

"Please tell me how is Vinita?" pleaded Prasad to one of the nurses who came out.

"Please have patience sir. Doctors will update accordingly."

"If there is any need to take her to some bigger hospital, please tell me. Money is no restriction."

"Prasad ji, we all know about it. Only the doctor can update how the patient is. I have to fetch few things urgently." She went away running.

They kept waiting for another hour. It was difficult to wait endlessly. Rakesh saw that Bhim sitting in a corner. He said, "Bhim uncle, I think you should leave now."

Prasad asked, "Did you see who those people were, Bhim?"

"Yes sir, I remember them properly. But I have not seen them here before."

"I will ask the police if they can make a sketch of the persons with your help."

"Sure sir. I would be glad to help in any way possible." Bhim indeed was. Years ago, his wife had complained that a neighbor was troubling her constantly and making lewd gestures. Bhim had confronted the man. The man had denied the charge squarely but Bhim killed him in a fit of rage. He was charged with this murder almost two decades back. Subsequently, when he went out on parole, he learned that his wife herself was an infidel. He sensed that probably the person he had killed was also telling him the truth. Maybe it was the other way round and he was spurning the advances that his wife was making. That possibly had made his wife furious and she had complained. His wife had left him for another person. Upon realizing that he had probably murdered by mistake, he took to penance inside the prison. His behavior improved dramatically and Prasad had taken up his case for an early release. The court had reduced his sentence. Bhim was released almost a decade back. But then, he did not have any place to go. Prasad had deployed him in his garden. Bhim used to sleep in Prasad's house. He was a great help. He was really sad that he could not save Vinita. He would do anything to help this family.

"Rakesh!" Bhim called him aside. He continued, "I did not tell Prasad ji. I have been with criminals for a very long time. I am sure that these two men have done this intentionally. My sense is that they are from Bardah."

Rakesh did not say anything but kept looking at Bhim. Till now, he had only been thinking about what could happen to him if he got involved with Vikram's gang. But the thought that this was now hurting his family made him very nervous. Earlier, they had hurt Ramu. And now his mother. He started sweating.

"Prasad ji. Come inside." One of the doctors called him.

Rakesh also went along. "The patient is still not out of danger. She is stable but still unconscious. The knife had ruptured her cervical nerve. I will be honest with you. Next few hours are really critical." Rakesh started crying. Prasad could also not hold on. He removed his glasses and wiped his eyes.

"Sorry, dad. It is all because of me. I should not have interfered. I will never forgive myself if anything happens to mother."

Prasad could not understand.

Rakesh continued, "Bhim uncle was saying that he believes that this was a deliberate act, most probably by the men from Bardah."

Prasad could not control his tears. He fell down on the floor. Rakesh and few others, who had come along, quickly lifted Prasad from the ground and made him sit on the bench nearby. Rakesh was also crying uncontrollably.

After almost three more hours, the doctors had some update. "I have some good news and some bad news for you. The good news is that madam is alive and stable. But the bad news is that…you have to be strong Prasad ji… Madam has gone into a coma. The damage to the cervical nerve had been severe."

Prasad was aghast. "What? How long will she remain in coma? Is there nothing that medical science can do? You know that money is not a problem. I can take her to the best of the doctors anywhere in the world. Please tell me!"

"Prasad ji, I wish there was a better answer. There is no proven treatment of a patient in coma. It may vary from several days to several weeks. Her health is stable otherwise. But we need to take extra care. Since she cannot respond, we have to ensure that she does not attract any of the common diseases which may worsen her health. We may keep her in the hospital or we may also keep her at home but with a trained nurse all around."

"Then we will take her home. At least she would hear familiar voices. Perhaps that will have a positive impact."

Chapter 30

Friends Check in on Rakesh

"Prasad ji, if you kindly allow me, I want to say something," pleaded Bhim with folded hands the next day at home.

"What is it Bhim?"

"I can understand what you might be going through. She is the pillar of this house. She has never harmed anyone. In the last two decades, I have thought so many times about the man I murdered. What exactly was his mistake? I killed him for something that he never did! Why did God allow this to happen to him? I have always wondered. Honestly, I have not found any answer even today. At times, fate has different things in store for us. Either it is the karma of our previous birth that catches with us, or it is a small piece of a much larger puzzle that is likely to unfold in the future. Both are not in our hands. You know, when I realized that I had murdered by mistake, it shook me from within. All I have been able to conclude is that we should continue our good work and forgive ourselves and others. But we should not forget things and try our best that we do not repeat any mistake in the future."

Prasad did not fully understand what Bhim was trying to conclude. But he knew that Bhim had gone through a very troubled phase and the more you go through fire, the wiser you become. He had always respected Bhim for his advice on life.

"I do not know how to say. But you should not blame Rakesh for all this. It has just been a strange turn of events and Rakesh has become involved in this. But we all know how much he loves you two. He would never do anything which would put any of you in danger. Please do not hold him responsible."

"Bhim, I know what you are saying. Yesterday, I was really angry when he told me that those men were probably from Bardah. We have always lived in fear of such things due to my profession. But never have I said no to any case because of any threat. And Vinita has always stood with me. I have been thinking about it. I do not know what I would have done if I were in place of Rakesh. Now, we have to be very careful. I do not want any risk to Rakesh. I have been thinking. Should I send him to some far-off place? What do you think?"

"Prasad ji, I think it is a good idea. Till the time things are sorted out here, we can send Rakesh to some far-off place where there won't be any risk of harm to him."

"But where can we send him? Who can stop few mavericks from finding out his whereabouts? It would not take much time for them to find out his location? And then you know what they might do to him!"

"Yes, you are right," said Bhim with a sad face.

The next day - tring, tring…

The phone at Rakesh's house rang. The servant answered, "This is Prasad ji's house. Who is this?" But there was no answer. He went off for his work. After another five minutes, the phone rang. Prasad was near and he picked up, "Hello. Who is this?" Again, there was no answer. He asked again, "Who is this? Whom do you want to speak to?" But the person on the other side simply hung up the phone. Probably someone had dialed a wrong number. Bhim called him outside for some work. As he went the phone rang again... Rakesh picked up the phone this time, "Hello. Who is this?"

"Hi, it is me." That feminine voice was what Rakesh had been missing badly all this time. His eyes became watery.

"Hi. How are you Nirmala?" Rakesh let out a long sigh.

"I heard about what happened. I feel so bad that I have caused so many problems to all near me. I wanted to come and see your mother. But I am literally under house arrest now."

"I can understand. My mother is in coma. We do not know when she would recover. Doctors have no clue. How are things at your end?" Rakesh was hoping that nothing unusual had happened at her place. But he was not sure. The goons were ruthless and unstoppable. He had already seen their wrath on his family.

"All is fine here. I am really surprised as to why would they attack your family. From the conversation I heard, the foreigner had strictly warned Vikram not to venture around me till his task was completed. And it seemed as if Vikram genuinely required at least six months for the task to be completed. I hoped that we had some time to figure out what exactly to do. I was completely shocked to hear about your mother. I am really sorry…" It was hard to control her tears.

And Rakesh understood. "I guess there are so many of his sympathizers that it would be difficult to control. Is there anyone around you?"

"Yes, I am at the phone booth. Why?"

"No, just take care of yourself. I will see you soon. Please do take care of yourself." Rakesh had always wanted to be with Nirmala. But these were tense times. He did not want her to be away from her home for long.

"You too. Thanks for everything. I hope this ends soon," said Nirmala before setting down the receiver.

Shakti came to visit Rakesh and his family. He was almost in tears. Rakesh, Binod and he had been childhood friends and Vinita had almost been like a mother to Binod and him as well. Numerous times, he had eaten with Rakesh at his home.

"I can't see aunty like this. What does the doctor say," asked Shakti.

"She is in a coma. No one can do anything now. We just have to wait and watch. Doctor don't say anything. But I am sure that with our care at home, she will recover soon. She is very strong from inside having witnessed so many threats due to papa's practice over the years. She has always stood like a pillar for this family," said Rakesh.

Shakti folded his hands in prayer. "Let us hope for the best. My father was also threatened. We are not sure who those people were. But I guess, they would also be from Bardah only," said Shakti in a low voice.

"I am sorry Shakti. Just because of me, our families are into trouble. But honestly, I don't even know what to do now. It is so difficult going through all these things," said Rakesh with eyes down and one hand on Shakti's shoulders.

Shakti pulled him closer, "Don't worry. There is nothing we could have done differently. Let us think about the future course of action. We have to think how to keep us and our families safer from all this. Mother has asked me to return before evening. I will leave now. If there is anything, please do give me a ring."

When Shakti had gone, Bhim pulled Rakesh closer, "Those two men were indeed from Bardah. But strangely, they have been knocked down by a truck yesterday. I got to know from my sources. Although it appears that it was just another incident of rash driving, it looks very strange. I guess it was a deliberate act. The police have not found anything about the owner of the truck. I hear that it was probably a stolen one."

Rakesh was surprised to hear that. Who could have killed them? Could it be his father? He loved his mother very much. These goons had endangered her life. He knew a lot of criminals through his practice. But his father probably would not stoop so low. Could it be Nirmala? But she was not so ruthless. Or was she? After all, she did kill three of Vikram's men when they had abducted her! Could it again be her this time? Or is it linked to the discussion that Nirmala had overheard between Vikram and the foreigner. The foreigner had asked Vikram to concentrate on his incomplete task for next six months. Could it be so that the foreigner found out about this incident and had punished Vikram's men for this?

Whatever it was, they had been punished adequately for what they had done to his mother. He was happy about it.

Suddenly, the phone rang again. Rakesh came to pick the receiver, "Who is this?"

"Hi Rakesh, it's me, Binod. How are you? It has been a long time!" the voice on the other side was of his dear friend. "And how is our Pandit ji?"

Rakesh was so happy to hear Binod's voice. He really missed Binod. He was one of the sharpest minds he had come across and he would definitely be of great help in the situation that they were in. But as a true friend, he did not want to put Binod's life in danger. He would not say a word of what had happened.

Clearing his throat, Rakesh managed to change his demeanor fast, "Hey, so nice to hear from you! We are all doing fine here. How are you doing these days?"

"I am fine, dear. How was your tryst at Sita Kund. Neither you nor Shakti bothered to tell me anything about it. Did you get to meet Nirmala? Did you get to talk?"

Rakesh was about to answer when he heard Bhim shout, "Rakesh baba, Prasad ji, come soon!"

Rakesh got tensed, "Listen Binod, I got to leave now. I will call you in a few minutes". Without waiting for Binod's response, he kept the receiver. He was worried what had happened now. But as soon as he entered the bedroom from where he had heard Bhim's voice coming, he was relaxed to see a beaming Bhim pointing towards his mother. His father was already by her bedside, with one hand over her head. Tears rolling down his cheek, Bhim said, "I just saw your mother opening her eyes. After Prasad ji came, she again closed her eyes."

This was indeed good news! Rakesh also started crying. He sat down beside his father. He was afraid that he would be cursing him for all the trouble that had fallen on the family. He found a hand gently caressing his hairs.

"How are you going to face this if you start crying? You need to be brave. We must think of how to handle this. I am going to meet the collector today. Let us see what he says."

After just a few minutes, the phone rang again. Rakesh picked up the phone. "Hi, is that Rakesh?" asked the impatient voice asked.

Rakesh knew the voice, "Yes, Binod. Sorry, I forgot to call you back. How…?" Before he could even complete his sentence, a worried sounding Binod shouted back, "What on earth has happened? I had a word with Shakti. He said that you guys are in some trouble? Look, he could not tell me everything. Somehow the phone got disconnected. What is happening? Tell me or else I am coming there myself tomorrow. My father had also told me few days back that there was some law and order problem again at Sita Kund. But he said that it was only a small thing and I need not worry about it. Why was Bhim shouting? In so many years, I have never heard him talking in a tone that could be heard more than five steps away."

Shakti, Binod and Rakesh had grown together. They had been a pillar of strength for each other. Rakesh had tried his best not to involve Binod in this matter in particular. In fact, he was sad that even Shakti's family was in trouble. But the brave front that he had kept in front of Binod trying not to reveal anything broke away finally. "What exactly did Shakti tell you?"

"He could just tell that you both have been involved in some trouble and from whatever little I could hear, I think it is connected with the incident at Sita Kund that my father had told me about a few days back. Now are you going to tell me all or do I have to find out myself? Damn it, I am worried now. Tell me fast!"

It is said that if you share a deep bond with someone, distances do not weaken the sense of feelings that people go through. Binod could just sense the trouble at the other end of the phone.

With a heavy sigh, Rakesh then poured out his heart to Binod.

❊ ❊ ❊

Chapter 31

A Mysterious Enquiry Begins

"Hello! Is this Patna Police Head Quarter?" A coarse voice asked on the phone.

"Yes?"

"I am a consultant from Security & Intelligence. We have been hired by the Chief Minister's office to create a new digital database for the State. I am doing a survey for the same. I would appreciate if you can answer them quickly. We are not asking your name. So be sure that whatever you say would be completely anonymous. We are not putting any name across the survey."

"Yes, sir. I am ready. Please go ahead." The caller could hear the screeching sound of the policeman's chair against the floor. He had stood up in attention. How could he ignore a call from a consultant hired by the Chief Minister's office?

"What digital database do you currently use?"

"We use the Crime and Criminal Tracking Network and System sir."

"Such a long name! Do you guys have any acronym for that?"

"We call it the Crime Net in short."

"Who all are authorized to see into Crime Net?"

"This is only for the senior people here."

"Do you have the privilege to check the Crime Net?"

"No, sir. I am only an inspector. I am not allowed to see. It is highly confidential."

"Not even inadvertently or on the order of your seniors?"

"No ,sir! Absolutely not! Mostly, Chand sir, our Deputy Commissioner only uses the system." The inspector was sweating as if he was almost caught doing a major crime himself.

"Do you not get to enter data of any crime? Is that also done by Chand?"

"No, no. That he asks us to do. But entering the data gives access only to a small part of the database. We all have our user names. We can just see the data that we enter. Only DCs and above have access to the entire database."

"How about police stations across other cities? Do they also have access to the database?"

"They do. But they also have restricted access. They can see only the data that they have entered. But they can request for access to other parts of the database. Once they receive the approval, they are able to view it."

"I see. Thank you very much. You have been of great help. I will mention in my remarks that you have helped me with lots of details. The Chief Minister's office regularly sees my comments and awards those who have been of help in the survey. What did you say your name was?"

"Prabhat Sharma, sir!" the policeman blurted out smiling happily. Who does not like a pat on his back?

And back at his institute, Binod was smiling too. It was easy to get the number of the Patna police head quarter on the internet. A clever thinking and a phone call from a pay phone had given him so much information for his next move.

"Hello! Is this Patna police head quarter?"

"Yes. What is it?"

"I am calling from Bengal Chief Minister's office. My name is Banerjee. Put me through to Chand." The heavy voice at the end of the line sounded authoritative. It was not a request; it was an order.

Moments later, "Hello sir, this is Chand speaking."

"Chand, this is Banerjee from Bengal Chief Minister's office. Your Chief Minister's office has given us your number. Our interceptors have come across a name and we want you to run a query against that. Just some usual stuff like what crimes does this name figure against? My people say that he might be up to something serious. Can you quickly open your Crime Net and check it for me? I am holding the phone."

"Yes…yes sir. I have logged in."

"Check for Vikram Yadav and tell me the latest crimes he is tagged onto. I have another meeting with your state's Chief minister this evening. I need to know that for our discussion."

"Yes sir. Vikram has been tagged onto several dreaded crimes. His name is tagged on to the recent arms smuggling at Bardah where he seems to have escaped. He is…"

"Listen, Chand. I am in a hurry. Can you just tell me the names of the crimes?" The voice grew impatient this time.

Chand was nervous. "AK-47 arms smuggling at Bardah, Maoist insurgency at West Midnapore, attack at Gaya, blast at Champaran, Purulia arms case, murder of..."

"Just tell me the bigger ones. I am not interested in murders, rapes etc. Is there any prominent person whose murder he is involved in?" The voice sounded a bit angry this time.

Chand could feel beads of perspiration on his forehead, despite the air conditioning. "No sir, there is a long list of other things, but they seem smaller in magnitude."

"Okay. I will tell your Chief Minister that you have been of help."

The called didn't express any gratitude. Chand was happy that the call was over and that he had not infuriated Mr. Banerjee. Who wants to be in the bad books of the Chief Minister? That would mean a long-lasting set back to his career!

And Binod was happy too. Masquerading as a caller from chief minister's office of the nearby state and dropping acronyms, it was easy to dupe Chand in believing that he was a genuine caller. Chand would never have the guts to cross-check. There would be at least 4-5 Banerjee in the chief minister's office at Bengal. After all, this was a very common surname!

❁ ❁ ❁

Chapter 32
Munger Police Station

"Is this Munger's main police station?" Binod had quite a handful of information from his last two calls for the next move.

"Yes, what happened? It is difficult to get some rest these days. What do you want?" The policeman behind the line appeared irritated and somewhat angry.

"I do not pay you to rest, you moron! What is your name?" The caller said in an angry tone.

"Sorry…sorry sir, I am Constable Ramesh!" The low-level policeman could hardly mutter realizing his mistake.

"This is Chand calling from the Patna police head quarter. Is this the way you behave on duty? Connect me to your senior right now. I will have you suspended immediately!" roared the voice on the other end.

"I beg you to pardon me, sir. It has been a long and exhaustive day and I just got carried away. I promise you that I will never behave like that again in my life."

"Ramesh, I know that sometimes we are under stress. But we are public servants. It is our duty to protect our society.

If we behave harshly, who will come to us to complain? If people stop complaining against criminals, then we would not be required anymore!" Binod softened his voice a bit. After all, a constable who was under obligation of being pardoned by a senior officer from the head quarter would be of great use.

He continued, "I need some information. Looks like the Crime Net is not working properly at our end. I know you guys keep physical records also. I need some urgent information on Vikram Yadav. I need information regarding few cases- AK-47 arms smuggling at Bardah, Maoist insurgency at West Midnapore, attack at Gaya, blast at Champaran, and Purulia arms case. Pull out all that you find. I will call you same time tomorrow."

Binod continued, "And listen. Do not take unnecessary stress. I will forget how you behaved in the beginning. But this work is very important. Do not discuss it with anyone, not even your colleagues and seniors. There is an urgent query involving Chief Minister's office and we do not want people talking about it. If I ever hear that you talked to anyone else, you know that our conversation is recorded. I will pull it up and you would be history."

"No sir. I promise…"

Even before he finished, the line had been cut from the other side.

❀ ❀ ❀

Chapter 33

More Information

"Put me through to Ramesh." The heavy voice at the other end was authoritative.

"Ramesh here. Who is this?"

"Ramesh, this is Chand. Have you noted down everything?"

Ramesh was excited. He had been up all night to fish out every detail he could find on the mentioned names. He would share all the information and make up for the bad behavior to such a senior person.

"Yes, sir. Which one should I start with?"

"Start with the latest incident first." Asked Binod who had masqueraded as Chand. His cleverness was bearing fruit.

'Sir, the latest incident is the AK-47 smuggling case. You know that there was a large cache of arms dropped in there."

"Yes, go ahead. I want to refresh my memory so that I know all the stuff for my meeting with the Chief Minister's office. The Crime Net is still not running here. I will ensure that you are rewarded for your help."

"Thank you, sir. You are ..."

"Ok, quick now. I have lot of work to do Ramesh. What does the file say about the AK-47 smuggling case?" Binod masquerading as Chand cut him in between. A tinge of authority was important to be kept all along.

"January 1996 – the police had got a tip off about large cache of AK-47 changing hands at Bardah. During the raid, a total of six AK-47 were confiscated. It appears that no one was caught red-handed. Three persons had been detained for questioning. After a lot of questioning, one of them had mentioned the name of Vikram Yadav. But then nothing much was found. They had been let go off after three days."

"Prior to this one was the Purulia arms case. This one is big." Ramesh continued. "A plane full of arms had been dropped off in Purulia. The plane was Antonov An-26 and had flown at a lower height to avoid detection. The police had found a large cache of arms and ammunition in 1995. Several hundred AK-47 assault rifles and several thousand rounds of bullets had been dropped. Luckily, the locals had informed the police and the police seized the same. Several days later, the aircraft re-entered the Indian airspace and was intercepted by Indian Air Force."

"The airplane was registered in Latvia. It had five Latvian citizens. There was a British person and another mercenary. They were captured. One of them had mentioned the name of Vikram Yadav as the key supplier of the cache. The file says that a raid had been organized by the central intelligence but Vikram Yadav was not found. There is not a word on who was the recipient of the cache. Since Vikram is from Bardah, the incident is written in detailed in the file here. The jurisdiction nonetheless is in West Bengal."

Binod was listening carefully. He did not need to take notes. He had a photographic memory. He could hear Ramesh flipping pages on the other side.

"What else do you have on this one?" Binod asked.

"Sir, there is a remark entered as of March 1996 in the same file. It says that Vikram Yadav had gone into hiding after that."

"Only that?"

"Sir, it says that he went into hiding under the pressure of his clients. There is another entry below that of 13th January 1997. It says that Vikram has been spotted in Bardah."

"Any word on why he had vanished into oblivion in 1996?"

"N,o sir. There is no mention of anything else on this incident. But I hear that he had done some goof up in Purulia because of which his client was angry. He was under pressure due to something related with that."

"Prior to that, there is some mention of him being associated in Naxal movements. In 1993, the file mentions that he was involved in supplying arms to Maoists for the Midnapore insurgency. Few local made small arms were caught being smuggled to West Midnapore. Again, no one was caught. It mentions informers as source saying that Vikram was the supplier."

"Prior to that, in 1990, there was an attack at Gaya police station. This appears to have linkage with caste wars. Once again, no one was captured. One of the detainees for questioning had revealed that Vikram's right hand was involved in supplying the crude bomb. There is a small remark dated March 1991 on this page which says that the right-hand man was killed in some gang war."

"The last one is the blast at Champaran. It says that some drug peddlers had caused a blast due to dispute with some local men. This was in 1989. It says that Vikram was the one involved in supplying the two revolvers that were left behind in that melee."

"Then there are some other older mentions…something about Nepal in 1988…then even earlier in Bangladesh in 1986…"

"That would be all. I hope the Crime Net is up and running soon. Else I have to call up people around. Anyways, I will keep your name in mind."

"Thank you very much, Chand sir!" said Ramesh. He noted that there was no "Thank You" at the end of the sentence. But he was really happy that the discussion had ended. He was glad that he had been awake the whole night and provided Chand sir with requisite information. Hopefully, Chand sir would forget about the initial casual remarks that he had made!

Chapter 34

Shakti's Father gets in Trouble

"Shakti, help!" Shakti's father, Dubey ji screamed out for his son as two men flung him into the Ganges. Shakti had gone to the Ganges along with his father to take bath in the Holy Ganges in the morning. Shakti was still enjoying the cold water while his father had come out and was offering prayers at the bank of the river. Two men had come from behind and lifted Dubey by force. Dubey was unable to understand anything. He was alarmed and kept asking as to what they wanted. Within no time, they carried him to the pillar from which kids used to jump into the water almost ten feet below. They simply swung him into the water and ran away.

Although Dubey had also lived all his life at the bank of the Ganges, he did know how to swim, but did not enjoy it and was not an expert. He went almost four feet inside the cold water.

Shakti was still inside the water. Hearing his father's cries, he quickly swam to save him.

H carried him to the steps. A lot of water had gone inside his father's lungs. He was unconscious. Shakti did not know what to do. He was very nervous. He checked his pulse. His pulse was running. Shakti was relieved.

"Anyone here? Please help me," he shouted several times. Few of the people from the temple came running. They pressed his chest and tried to revive him. Slowly, Dubey showed signs of movement.

Shakti was relieved. He along with others carried his father to his home. His mother started crying seeing her husband in this condition.

"What happened to your father?"

"Someone threw him from above into the Ganges," said Shakti.

They made Dubey lie down on the cot. He had gained more strength by that time.

"How is you dad?" asked Shakti. Tears were still rolling down his cheek.

His father raised his hands conveying that he was better.

One of the men asked, "Shakti, did you see who those people were?"

"No, I turned that side when I heard dad scream. I only saw two people running away on the pillar there."

Dubey coughed. "Ah, Shakti!"

"I am here only dad. How are you now? I am calling a rickshaw and we will take you to the doctor."

"No, no. I am fine now. I just drank a plenty of water." He moved and Shakti's mother helped him to sit straight.

"Do you know any of the ones that pushed you?" asked one of the men who had helped in carrying him home.

"I did see them. But I have not seen them before. I do not know why they pushed me down. They did not say a word."

It is said that a woman's intuition is the strongest. Shakti's mother said, "They must be from Bardah."

Shakti could feel goose bumps all over his body. He could feel beads of perspiration on his forehead even in the slightly cold weather.

His mother continued, "Even Rakesh's mother had been assaulted by people from Bardah. What is God punishing us for?" She was crying hysterically.

Chapter 35

Binod gets Gutsy

Binod was happy that he had been able to fish out important information about Vikram.

So, the information suggested that the most recent was the Purulia arms drop case. Prior to that, he had been involved in several cases with Naxals. Most cases appeared related to arms smuggling. Purulia incident by far appeared the most dangerous involving thousands of arms and ammunition.

He tried to focus on what else Shakti had told him on the phone. Ah, Shakti had mentioned that Vikram had vanished into oblivion after the first kidnapping of Nirmala! That matched with what the police diary mentioned. He tried to remember each and everything that Shakti had told. He recalled that when Nirmala was in captivity, she had seen a foreigner who had ordered Vikram to focus on the pending work. So probably the foreigner was his client or his boss. But then, Shakti had also mentioned that there was some clash between the men of Vikram and those of the foreigner. That meant that the foreigner was not his boss but his client.

"Bingo!" He said to himself. From the information he had, Purulia arms drop case was the only one which involved a non-Asian foreigner. Although Vikram was involved in cases in Nepal and Bangladesh as well as per the police files, one would not classify a person from those countries as a foreigner just by looking.

"It definitely is the Purulia arms case in which he and the foreigner are related. Probably he did not complete his task properly and that is the reason why he goes into hiding," he said to himself.

But what task could that be? He was already into hiding for almost a year before the second kidnapping of Nirmala! Now also, he seemed to have asked for more time to complete the task. The client had given him six months. What could it be?

He had already gathered a lot of information on him from the state records. How can he find more?

He had an idea…

"Hi, CBI Head Quarters. How may I help you?"

"Hi. My name is Prahlad Sharma. I am calling from West Bengal. I had actually met Pooja ma'am from HR for an interview last week. She had asked me to send my pay slips to her so that she can make me an offer. She had also asked for some recommendations for referral checks. I have some query on that. Can you please connect me to her?"

"Sure. What name did you say?"

"It is Pooja something. I do not remember her last name."

"Let me check. Sorry, there is no one by the name of Pooja in the HR department. Are you sure this was the name?"

"Actually, there were three persons in the interview. I thought she introduced herself as Pooja. She is a young girl probably in her late twenties. I seem to be confused on the name now! Can you please help me with whatever name you find in the directory for HR? Just give me some junior person. It would not be wise to put some small queries to seniors."

"Sure. There are two names- Anita and Sneha. Whom would you like to speak to?"

"Ma'am, my son is getting cranky. My wife is not at home right now. If I do not tend to him right away, he will fall off the bed. Can you please give me the extension of Anita ma'am so that I can call her after some time directly?"

"Yes. It is 1359. Anything else?"

"No. Thanks a lot. I am sure going to catch up with you once I join there. I must say that you have a lovely voice! What did you say your name was?"

"My name is Julie, Hope to see you soon dear!" Julie was smiling as she put down the phone. She was glad that she had helped someone who was to join there soon. In fact, she helped quite a lot of people. That's what her job was! But it was rare that anyone appreciated her.

Binod had managed to get the extension of Anita from HR department at the CBI head quarter.

"Hi. Is this Anita from HR?" Binod called after a little while.

"Yes. Who is this?"

"Good afternoon. This is Jack. I am from Info Consulting. We are installing some updates on all the computers in the investigation department. Listen, I have an urgent request and someone suggested you could help."

"I am a bit busy. But tell me. What is it about?"

"We have to complete this task by today evening. You know how bosses are. He just informed me a little while ago that I need to complete the installations by the end of today. This fatty is so irrational. He did not even wait for my reply. Now that I started doing, I realize that there are a couple of people who are out for meetings. I can still contact them and get around completing my installation for them. But what about the ones that are on leave and not even reachable? One of the friendlier guys said that I could request you. I swear that if I do not complete the work today, this fatty would fire me left right and center."

"I know. It is very difficult to work with irrational bosses." Binod had won her sympathy. Who has not experienced a bad boss after all!

"Thanks a lot, Anita. You are really kind. I will not take much of your time. Can you give me a list of the people who are on leave? Against each person, I would also need the name of his neighbor and the neighbor's extension so that I can get some help from them. Even if they login as a guest, then also I would be able to install the patch."

"Ok. Three persons from the investigation team are on leave- Prabhakar Rao, Krishna Kant and Harshad Jhaveri. Prabhakar Rao sits next to Joseph, extension 7274. Krishna sits next to Preeti, extension 3433 and Harshad sits next to Sonia, extension 9867. Prabhakar seems to be on a block leave and won't be returning for another fortnight."

"Thanks a lot, Anita. You have been really kind. When I have to install these for the HR team, I will make sure that I help you first. If you ever have any problem, I mean computer problem, you can bank on me for help."

"Thanks. Hope you can complete your work in time!"

"Yes, sure. You have been of great help. These days, bosses treat employees like shit. I do not know how long will I last here!"

"I am sure you will do well. I have to go now, got to do some work, yeah?"

"Sure. Thanks once again."

It was the time for the next move.

"Joseph, this is Prabhakar here. You got a minute?"

"Prabhakar? You sound so different? I thought you were on holiday? What happened?"

"Joseph, I am out in some remote area now and the signal is really bad here. I am calling from a phone booth. Listen, one of my agents updated me on a case. I am trying to relate which case this could be related to. I fear that this could be something big. I have a hunch that it might be connected to one of the cases. But I have been so busy handling kids and wife and arranging things for the holiday that my head is spinning. I have not been able to sleep yesterday night. I am not able to concentrate. I need your help in sort of refreshing my memory on that case."

"I know how you are feeling man. We have to work at office, do all shit. Then go home and the family is waiting anxiously for you to entertain them. We poor husbands!"

"Yes. Terrible. I want to end this quickly before my kids are awake. We are back from a tiring day and they are sleeping. You know about this Purulia arms drop case?"

"Yes, the mysterious unsolved one. Let me login into the database. Tell me what you want to know. Hey, but was not Amit on this case?"

Binod was prepared. "Yes, I know, but actually I am not sure if my hunch is right. So I just want to refresh whatever is available right now and work on that to check my hypothesis. If my hunch is right, then only I will speak to him. Else why complicate an already complicated case?"

"True, buddy. Tell me what you want to know."

"Listen, if I remember correctly, there was a huge cache of arms dropped. There were few foreigners involved, I guess from Latvia and also a British if I am not wrong."

"Yes, Correct. But the record here says that the Latvian or the Russian had run away."

"Yes, right. Who all are the possible recipients of the cache mentioned there?"

"It says that the arms could be for Anand Marg or for the agents of the central government itself to disrupt peace in order to create problems for the ruling CPI (M) party."

"Any names mentioned there? The Latvians/Russians or the British? Oh, I am so tired that I can't recall names from such a famous case!"

"It happens man. Take it easy. You need to rest. And the holiday doesn't seem like helping you. The Russian's name is Kim Davy and the British guy's name is Peter Bleach."

"No, I mean I remember the names, any nicknames mentioned against these guys?"

"Yes, Kim is also called Krem or Dorov or Alexander. I do not see anything against Peter though."

"It is mentioned that he has been in and out of India, last spotted only few days back…in a place named Bardah. Looks like our bureau has a birdie on him!"

What's a birdie? Binod did not know the jargon. But he dared not show his ignorance.

"Really? What does it mention?"

"It says number thirteen, nothing else."

"Ok, leave it. I guess I will work with that. Ah it looks like someone's on the door. Listen I got to go now. The bell would wake up my wife and kids. Bye."

Binod let out a big sigh of relief as he cut the call. He had managed to hide his nervousness on the phone. But it was difficult. He was trying to sneak information from the highest-ranking investigating agency of the country. He wiped the few beads of perspiration that had come on his forehead.

He had made all the calls to the CBI using his computer. Multilayered network of routers and a virtual private network concealed the identity of his computer. Besides, he had carefully chosen to masquerade as Prabhakar. The HR had already mentioned that he would not be in for another fortnight as he was on a block leave. He had finally been able to regain his composure.

Chapter 36
Binod Rings Rakesh

"Hi, can I speak to Rakesh?"

"Hi Binod. It's me."

"So how are things there? How is aunty doing?"

"Mom is doing fine. She has started to make some movements. Doctors say this is most incredible. They have never seen such a fast recovery from coma. They just don't know what steel she is made up of!"

"I am so glad dear," Binod felt a sigh of relief. "Listen carefully…"

Binod then narrated in brief what all information he had collected. He was careful that no one was snooping around.

"This is really great!" Rakesh was not able to understand how Binod managed to find so much. But he knew that Binod was the most intelligent among the three friends. He could always come up with something when others had given up.

"I think we would need some external help, Rakesh. Beyond this, we need some action on the field. Can you connect me to Bhim?"

"I will ask him to give you a call. When should I ask him?"

"Ask him to call my hostel's reception and ask for me tomorrow afternoon. From a pay phone."

❁ ❁ ❁

Chapter 37
Bhim at Help

"Hi. Can I speak to Binod please?"

"Yes. Binod here. Who is this?"

"Binod, this is Bhim. Is this a good time to call?"

"Sure. I need some help. This is regarding Rakesh. And this has to stay only between you and me. Please do not even tell it to Rakesh or Shakti. Things may go out of hand. I do not want them to be bothered unnecessarily. I will update them at appropriate time."

"Ok. Tell me."

"I have a name and I want to know more about it. The incident is related to Purulia and I think someone in the underground network in that location might know. At least we have to try. Possible to get some help?"

"Prasad ji has given me a new life. You know that I do not have anyone else apart from them. I am sure that I can find someone."

"Ok. I want to know about Kim Davy. He is also known by other names- Krem or Dorov or Alexander. Also, please find out what is the meaning of a birdie? Say, if someone says that the CBI has a birdie on Kim, what could it mean?"

"Ah, I know that one." He had stayed long in the prison to learn about the criminal world. "That means an informer."

"Ok. So please see if we can find anything about *thirteen* as well?"

"Eh, *thirteen*?"

"Yes, I think that could be a code name. I am afraid that we do not have anything more."

❊ ❊ ❊

Chapter 38
Digging in Purulia

"Hi, I am looking for Cheetah."

"Then you should go to some forest. There is no Cheetah here," said the man behind the cash register in the shop at Purulia, getting angry and alert suddenly.

"The jungle is flooded so I have come to look for the one with the horns," the man in the shop leaned ahead and signaled Bhim to keep quiet. He knew what the code meant.

He held Bhim's hand and took him inside the small door on the wall. The door led into a dimly lit store room. Bhim could see heaps of grocery kept inside- cartons of various kinds of food, soaps, cold drinks etc. The storeroom was not very large. The man moved a few empty boxes aside. A small door of say four feet high emerged on the carefully covered back wall. There was another person lying down in the storeroom. He quickly closed the door and covered it with the cartons as they emerged on the other side. They came out on the other side in what appeared like another house. There were few people inside the house doing their chores. The man accompanying Bhim bowed to one or two and kept going. There was another door on the right wall. A man was sitting near it on a stool. He bowed to the man with Bhim. There was a lock dangling on the door. "Who is this guy?"

"He wants to meet Cheetah," said the man accompanying Bhim. He opened the door and let them inside. There were two persons in the room doing some work. Bhim noted that these were very muscular. The man accompanying Bhim pulled the thick carpet on the floor. Bhim was surprised to see the small wooden door on the floor. Bhim felt that the man with him did something and the door fell down showing a staircase.

"Come down carefully."

After few steps, they emerged into a room which was more of a dungeon.

"Boss, this person wants to meet you."

The man in the front appeared a bulky five feet short guy. He hardly had any hairs on his head. Bhim noticed that his right ear was partly cut at the top. His eyes stuck there, trying to figure out what could have caused that.

Cheetah noticed it. "Have you seen dogs fighting? They often have their ears bitten by rivals. My entry to this world was also through a dog fight. Only that I had to fight a real dog. It was taller than me when it stood on its hind legs."

"But our boss was strong enough to kill it!" prompted the man who had brought Bhim to the dungeon.

Cheetah gave him a stern look. No one was supposed to talk when he was speaking. The man with Bhim stepped back with a guilty expression on his face. Bhim saw that he was sweating.

"So what have you come for Bhim?"

Bhim was surprised that Cheetah knew his name. "Sir, I am a friend of Malkan. We spent time together in prison for some time."

"I know. Malkan told me about it. He told me how you saved him several times from the fellow criminals. He likes you very much. Tell me. What do you want from me?"

"Dada. I myself was on life imprisonment. But I was reformed by a lawyer at Munger. I was later released due to my good behavior. Since then, I have been sort of adopted by that family. I do odd jobs at their house and also stay with them. They have been very kind to me."

"Malkan was telling me. Go on."

"The only son of the family got involved somehow with Vikram Yadav from Bardah…"

Interrupting Bhim, Cheetah said, "Yes, I know very well about him." He stood up from the slightly broken chair that he was sitting on. He had suddenly become very serious. His eyes were looking miles away.

"Leave us alone. Do not disturb us for another half an hour," Cheetah asked other men in the room. Only Bhim was left. When others had left, he asked Bhim, "What exactly do you want?"

"Dada, it seems that Vikram vanished few days back. There seems to be some unfinished tasks for which he has gone into hiding for next few months. Our understanding is that this is about the Purulia arms drop case. We are not actually bothered what is he involved with. But when he comes back, we fear for the life of Rakesh, my boss' son. So we want to first know completely about Vikram. Then only we would be able to do anything."

"Bhim, I do not want to discourage you. But you know that when there is a goat in front of a lion, it is not what the goat does matters. The prerogative of 'doing' lies with the lion."

Bhim understood. But he was hoping that they would find something to nail him down. Probably not by force, but they might expose him in a way that even his connections would not be willing to save him. Prasad ji was an excellent lawyer. Even Binod had done brilliant work finding out so much about Vikram. Bhim knew that they were not strong enough. But when it came on one's life, even a common man could move mountains! He himself had developed some good acquaintances during his imprisonment.

"Dada, we do not have much choice. If we do not do anything, we are going to be killed. We are seeing next few months as an opportunity to nail him down. We need your help. Please."

Cheetah sighed. "What do you want from me?"

"We want to understand what exactly is this Purulia arms case all about? How is Vikram involved?"

"Vikram had promised to deliver a large cache of arms to some client of Kim Davy, a Russian criminal. It is still not clear as to who was the ultimate beneficiary. Few people have been rumored- Anand Marga, the central government itself. No one knows exactly who. Apparently, Vikram had sent his own pilot in the first instance. Looks like the pilot developed cold feet and dropped the cache randomly. That's why the police were able to find the cache. The pilot then went back and tried to flee. Vikram had gone into hiding fearing Kim. The pilot was killed by Kim. Kim flew back again in the same plane to see the place where the arms had been dropped. He was not aware that the arms had been caught and that his plane would be on a watch. He was intercepted and caught but he managed to flee."

"Kim had lots of connections. He fished out Vikram and gave him another year to deliver the arms to the ultimate beneficiary. But arranging such huge number is not an easy task. Plus, Vikram had taken quite a loss due to the seizure. From what I hear, he is again trying to arrange for the arms consignment. That is the reason why he has vanished from Bardah."

This made sense to Bhim. He suddenly found pieces of the puzzle falling into place. "Dada, anything more you know about Kim? I think he had also come to Bardah a month back."

"Look, Bhim. He is a very dangerous man. We are very small time compared to him. Even Vikram is small compared with him. It is difficult to find him. He comes in a flash and vanishes into thin air. He is very fond of technology and communicates mostly using internet."

"Dada, I also hear that CBI might be snooping on him."

"Could be true. I hear that he is on the top of their radar. This means that sooner or later, they would tighten their noose on him. I guess they are waiting to uncover the whole plot. Listen, Vikram is an adopted son. Although the Thakur who adopted him is confined to a wheel chair, Vikram still keeps him in loop for everything. May be if one is near to him, you may know better about what he is up to."

"Thanks, dada. I would bother you again if I need some help."

"Sure, Malkan is my boy. I will do whatever is possible. But be careful. There is death all along the way you have chosen."

Death was not something that was new to him. He had killed once and had almost defied death inside prison. What was life anyway if he could not help the one who helped him live another life - one of respect and love?

❁ ❁ ❁

Chapter 39
Next Move

"Binod!" Bhim turned back to see who had kept his hand on his shoulder. Binod had wrapped a shawl around him. Only his face was visible. They met inside the Surya temple. Bhim had rung up Binod to update him. Binod took the next train and had reached Purulia. It was hardly a four-hour journey from Kharagpur.

"What do we do now? We do not have much information!"

"What are you saying Bhim? You have done a wonderful job coming here! And we do have lots of information! What appeared sophisticated to Cheetah is actually the easiest way to zero in on Kim. If we have luck, we can even zero in on *thirteen*!"

"I do not know what you are talking about Binod!"

"It is very easy to find whereabouts on internet. If Kim communicates through internet, it would not take much time for me to track him down."

Bhim could not understand much. He was not so educated. He just nodded his head. They headed to a restaurant nearby.

It was deserted. They took the corner table. No one was around. Bhim saw that Binod was in a pensive mood.

"What are you thinking Binod?"

"We have to expose Vikram in such a way that the police are bound to catch him irrespective of how deep Vikram's connections are," said Binod in a low tone. "Dada, you can go back now. Please don't discuss any of this even with Rakesh. In the meantime, I will think of something. Let us go and eat something. I am really feeling hungry."

There was a small tea stall. They went there and ordered for tea and bought some biscuits to eat along. They hardly spoke about anything. Both were deep in their thoughts.

"Hi, can you hear me? This is Mitul from Purulia..." a man was almost shouting on the pay phone at the tea stall. Something attracted Binod towards him. He just kept staring. The man on the phone was turned the other way. Binod's eyes were hooked on to him. Bhim realized it after a while.

"What happened Binod?" asked a puzzled Bhim.

"Nothing, are you done with your tea? Let us go now," said Binod. As they walked along, Binod saw that there were not many people around. It was safe to speak. He said, "Dada, I have an idea. You have to go to Bardah and do some work for me." Bhim listened to Binod. He smiled and they parted.

Chapter 40
Bhim at Bardah

In broad day light, Bhim, covering his face with a fake beard and a big moustache, was roaming around in Bardah on a cycle. He had put on a bag and pretended to be a courier person. He was lazily cycling around and doing a recce of the village. He spotted just one telephone junction in Bardah. The very next day, Bhim dressed up as a telephone technician and opened up the junction in broad day light. He carried a phone and other tools with him. Who would suspect a technician working on a public telephone junction in broad day light?

He worked on the wires as directed by Binod. It appeared that there were only two telephone lines. He pierced open the wires and connected his phone to check. Both appeared working fine. He looked at the wires going out of the junction box. He carefully installed the bugs as Binod had directed. He then left the place. He would wait for another day for the next move.

After two days, he returned to the same spot dressed as an electrician. He had some wires around his shoulder. He climbed the thicker tree some distance away from the junction box. He pretended to be working with the wires. He waited to check if he had attracted anyone's attention. The place was all clear. Although it was winter, it was bright in the noon and people preferred staying indoors. He carefully took out what appeared like a bird's nest. He carefully put the radio receiver inside the nest and checked if it was working as instructed by Binod. Once satisfied, he came down and vanished from Bardah.

But he could not stay at Bardah for long. He returned to Rakesh's house. Vinita was recovering well. Although she was bed ridden, she had started moving her hands. She was still unable to speak but could communicate using hand gestures. There was no more violence for some reason.

After a week, Bhim went to Bardah again. This time too he dressed as an electrician. He first parked his cycle some distance away from the telephone junction box. He moved towards the junction box carefully. He kept looking around to check if anyone had any suspicion. Once again, he chose noon time for his work. There was nothing suspicious. He inspected the telephone booth. He had put a very thin wire across the door in such a way that while it stayed largely invisible, it would break as soon as someone tried to open the door. He was surprised to see it broken exactly as Binod had suggested.

He then moved towards the tree where he had hidden the radio receiver. He carefully put the receiver inside his bag, came down from the tree. He suddenly found a man underneath the tree looking at him. As he got down from the tree, the man asked, "Brother, what is the problem? When are you guys going to change the transformer? There are frequent cuts these days."

Bhim said, "That is what I have come for. I have been carrying out some inspections. Some wires also need to be changed. It is likely that the work would be carried out in next few days." He blurted out trying to keep a calm composure. Without waiting for a response from the person, he kept moving slowly so as not to arouse any suspicion.

He moved to another lane to avoid that person. Slowly he moved to his cycle and paddled away from Bardah. He breathed a sigh of relief. Hopefully, this was the last time he had to come to Bardah.

❀ ❀ ❀

Chapter 41

Binod Charts out the Next Step

Bhim had to give the radio receiver to Binod.

As Prasad picked up the receiver, "Can I speak to Bhim?" asked the voice on the other side. Prasad was surprised. In last so many years, not one single phone has come for Bhim. "Wait a minute, I am calling him." Bhim came running as Prasad called out for him.

"Hi, this is Bhim speaking," said Bhim. Next few minutes, he spoke only in monosyllables. But he appeared happy. As he put the phone down, he went to Prasad who was standing few steps away in the same hall.

"Sir, my brother just called. He had met me in the market a couple of days back. My niece is getting married in the village. Is it possible to get a leave of four days? It has been a long time since I met my folks. Things here look much better now. If you kindly permit me…"

"Sure, Bhim! I am happy for you. You must go. When do you want to leave?"

Bhim already knew that Prasad would not deny him the permission. "If it is fine, can I go today night itself?"

Prasad took out some money from his purse and handed it to Bhim, "Please buy some good gifts for the couple."

Bhim was reluctant to take it. After all, they treated him like his family. He anyway was paid his monthly wage. But he knew that he may need some since he was to go to Kharagpur by train and return. He took after some hesitating.

At night, he boarded a train to Calcutta and reached by the morning. At Calcutta, he bought a ticket to Kharagpur. The train from Calcutta to Kharagpur took another three hours. Just as the train stopped at Khargapur, he got out of station quickly. He saw a rickshaw standing. "Hey you, will you go to the IIT campus?"

"I am waiting to find a passenger for some other place. But if you insist, I will charge fifty rupees?"

Bhim knew that it was useless to bargain with the rickshaw pullers there. They were very arrogant and could start a fight on petty things. He just nodded in affirmative and boarded the rickshaw.

The rickshaw puller did not seem to be in any hurry. He was slowly pulling away. Bhim needed as much time as he could get. He said, "Brother, I will give you an extra ten bucks if you reach in another fifteen minutes."

The rickshaw puller then started driving fast. As soon as he reached the IIT campus, he saw a big entrance with iron gates and security guards at both sides. But no one asked anything. He saw the road inside covered with thick trees on both sides. It was a mesmerizing site. On the left side, he saw what looked like the main building of the institute. He was lost looking at the buildings nearby.

"Where exactly do you want to go my friend," asked the rickshaw puller. Bhim remembered that Binod had asked him to come to Nehru Hall, the hostel at which Binod was lodged in during his last year of study at the institute.

In next few minutes, Bhim reached a confluence of what looked like three hostels. He handed sixty rupees to the rickshaw puller. He happily rode away.

Bhim enquired and reached at the entrance of the hostel. At the reception, the watchman asked him to wait. He then shouted at few students who were going inside the hall to ask Binod to come to the reception.

In next 2-3 minutes, Binod came running to the reception. He took Bhim to his room and bolted it from inside. "Yes dada, did you bring it?"

Bhim took out the radio receiver carefully and handed it to Binod. Binod then took Bhim and the radio receiver to a computer lab. He attached one of the sockets which enabled the recorded conversation to be heard. Binod then put a headphone in order not to allow anyone else to listen to the conversation. Bhim patiently kept sitting on a chair next to Binod. He spent almost six hours doing something on the computer while listening to the conversations recorded in the receiver. A beaming Binod then took out the receiver and asked Bhim to accompany him outside. Binod took Bhim out to a nearby tea stall. On the way, he said, "Bhim, our efforts have been very successful. I found only two conversations which were encrypted. Whoever the number *thirteen* is, sent the first message to the CBI head quarter that Vikram is set to meet Kim and that he would get the exact location in some time. The second message from him was that the meeting would happen on 2nd April 1997 in Calcutta."

Bhim was astonished to see how Binod had been able to get so much information. He knew Binod since long and he was aware that Binod was studying in one of the most prestigious engineering institutes of the country. He could not hide his disbelief.

Reading his face, Binod said, "Dada, don't be surprised. I had already found out that there was some informer for CBI at Bardah. There are very few means that these spies use to communicate. Since not much option is available at Bardah, I zeroed in on the telephone junction box. As you saw, it is pretty easy for anyone to just tap into one of the existing telephone connections from there, connect to a desired number and communicate. That is the reason why we placed the bugs and the radio receiver. It is difficult for the CBI to do a periodic two-way communication with its birdie in a remote place like Bardah which does not even have power for the most of the times. So, it was obvious that the birdie or number *thirteen* needed to communicate with the CBI on a regular basis. Our hypothesis was that at least a weekly communication would be necessary. That's why we collected a whole week's conversations. Just ass I had thought, number *thirteen* would not communicate in normal language but an encrypted one. That is why I was able to crack our case so fast. There were just two communications which were gibberish- the first stretched just over two minutes while the second was slightly lesser than three minutes."

Bhim was still perplexed. He had heard about such things during his long years of imprisonment. He was aware of such things. But Binod was not a spy. He was just a student! How did he know so many things?

Binod said further, "It is pretty easy to decrypt messages once you have a computer with you. There are several algorithms, or what one may call procedures to dissect pats of conversation and try to make sense out of such encryptions. It is difficult, but not impossible. You know, I have already been selected in one of the companies and there is not much of a load these days. More importantly, Rakesh and Shakti are two precious friends. I know that had I been in trouble, they would not think twice in risking their lives if it could save me. And that is exactly what I have done. But as you have promised, all these conversations must remain between the two of us only. Please do not discuss it even with Rakesh or even Prasad uncle."

Bhim nodded, "So what next?"

Binod was busy thinking. He had twelve days more before 2nd April 1997. Kim and Vikram would meet at the Sea Lounge Restaurant just at Gate Number 6 exit of the Esplanade Station. The meeting was supposed to be at 6pm. The location ensured that if anything went wrong, both would vanish into the thick population in no time without being caught. The area was full of tourists anyway. No one would have a suspicion on that front.

He would think of something by that time. "I cannot let go of this chance," said a pensive Binod to himself.

❁ ❁ ❁

Chapter 42
The D-day

"Calcutta TV?"

"Yes?"

"Listen carefully," the voice on the other side said in a rough Bengali tone. "There is about to be a big scoop at the Hungry Restaurant outside the Esplanade Metro at 6pm. Don't miss out."

"Hello! What is it regarding?" almost shouted the person at Calcutta TV but the caller had already kept down the receiver. Binod was slightly nervous. This was a chance that could not be missed.

But just to ensure that he did not waste the chance, he did the same thing calling two more channels. This would ensure that just sufficient coverage. He did not want a lot of journalists with their vans to raise suspicion in minds of the targets. He deliberately gave the name of a restaurant which was just 50 meters away from the Sea Lounge Restaurant. It was a tourist place and it was normal to see one or two newspaper vans at such places.

He had had his lunch at the Sea Lounge Restaurant the previous day along with Bhim. Both had done a nice recce of the area. At 5 pm, they again met a little away from the restaurant.

"You think it will work," asked a worried Bhim. Binod too was nervous. But he knew that his plan was full proof, provided the two showed up. He just nodded. Both then went to the restaurant just opposite Sea Lounge. It was already 5:30 pm.

They had taken the table just at the exit so that they could see what was happening inside Sea Lounge. Both Binod and Bhim had managed to see Vikram and Kim's photo and they were pretty sure that they could spot both. As Binod was sipping his tea, Bhim drew his attention towards the other side of the road. Vikram could be seen walking towards Sea Lounge. Binod could feel his heart beat thumping much faster. It was one thing to snoop within the comfortable confines of his institute and entirely different piece of cake to execute something in person that too in such close vicinity of dreaded criminals. He became alert. Vikram appeared to have entered the restaurant alone. Although it could very well be that his men were already inside the restaurant or just walking nearby.

It was almost 5:50 pm. Both Bhim and Binod could feel beads of perspiration on their face. The already humid weather of Calcutta had made it worse. But at least it did not raise any suspicion.

Every now and then, Binod would look at his watch. By almost 5:58 pm, he saw a taxi stopping in front of the restaurant. A foreigner entered Sea Lounge. Both Binod and Bhim could not see his face.

"I need to take a peek," said Binod quickly rising from his chair.

Bhim did not say anything, but his eyes said it all, "Be careful." And Binod understood very well. He nodded in affirmative and proceeded quickly towards Sea Lounge. As he entered, he was relieved to see both Kim and Vikram sitting in front of each other on a table. They were not talking but looking into some documents. Binod quickly turned around and left the restaurant to find Bhim standing outside. They moved away from there to the other side of the road. Bhim looked at someone in the crowd and signaled something. The other person closed his eyes acknowledging that he had read the signal. The very next moment, there was a loud explosion inside the Sea Lounge restaurant.

There was confusion all around. It was not clear as to what had happened. It was a crowded place. It appeared that the explosion had happened inside Sea Lounge. People started running here and there randomly but away from Sea Lounge. Only four people were seen going towards ground zero. All had identity cards of different media houses dangling from their necks. Behind them were what appeared like their support staff with cameras and mikes. Within seconds, they heard loud siren of a police car. Suddenly the area turned into a fortress. There were police personnel everywhere. The whole area was cordoned off.

Bhim and Binod had taken seat in a restaurant little away. They had chosen this one as it had a television. As they were sipping their tea just twenty minutes post the explosion, it appeared that the incident was covered in several channels. Even those whom Binod had not called beforehand had reached the place and started giving live coverage. They could see the police catching a foreigner. Bhim and Binod could see that Kim had definitely been caught. However, they could not see Vikram being caught. There was a small interview that one of the policemen had given. He just told that one foreigner had been caught. He appeared to have met one of his accomplices there. But others escaped.

They could not believe their ears. They looked at each other. It appeared that Vikram had not been caught. They were sweating profusely. This meant that Vikram would definitely hunt for whoever created this mess. This only meant that death was lurking close.

Both hurriedly moved out of the place.

As they were walking, Binod said hurriedly, "Bhim dada, can you please check if Vikram has really escaped?" They spent the night in one of the smaller hotels. Bhim went out in the city and returned after a few hours.

"Binod, the news was correct. Only Kim has been caught. Vikram seemed to have escaped," Bhim said. Both were worried. They could not sleep the whole night. They had executed their plan well. As Bhim had directed, one of his older mates from the prison had exploded a special bomb inside Sea Lounge. The bomb was more of a hoax designed to create a loud decibel and some smoke in order to give the impression of a real bomb explosion. It being a crowded area, there was always some police contingent around. The presence of the media ensured that the police caught Kim in full glare of the media. They had calculated that in fact, both would be caught together. Having caught in front of cameras, police would then find it difficult to let go off the two.

But the plan had misfired with Vikram not in the net. Bhim and Binod looked into each other's eyes. Almost simultaneously, they said, "Let us go to Munger." They did not talk much after that. The night was still not over. They were tired, but there was no sleep in their eyes. Both understood very well that Vikram had been away from Bardah only because of Kim's threat regarding the pending delivery of arms. With Kim caught, his focus would again turn to Nirmala.

Both packed their bags and left for the railway station immediately. The train to Jamalpur, the nearest station for Munger, was still few hours away. Binod then rang Rakesh, "Be careful. He might be returning soon." Binod was feeling so embarrassed that despite all their efforts, he could not help his friends. In fact, he pre-poned the grave danger that was at least few months away and they could have done something better during that time.

Bhim read his thoughts. He said, "Don't blame yourself. We have tried our best. We must now focus on the future." At the back of his mind, he was hoping for some miracle which could keep his loved ones safe from the goons.

Chapter 43
Back at Munger

As soon as Bhim and Binod landed in Munger, they both went to Rakesh's house. Binod was sad to see Vinita on the bed. That also reminded him what could be in store for them in the coming days. This was a fight of a different level where there was no value for life. Honestly, they were no match for brawn. Even brain had failed them so far despite their best efforts. God knows what lay ahead.

"Look who is there!" exclaimed Rakesh upon seeing the two. Binod had not told him everything. He had just said that Vikram would be returning soon and that everyone should be careful. Rakesh was amazed at how Binod knew something like that. He had insisted for details but Binod knew that even Rakesh's phone could be tapped. He had kept the conversation brief.

Prasad was fond of Binod. In fact who would not be? After all, he was one of the best students in the town. He was also very focused and not involved in any of the normally considered ill habits of youth. He was filled with joy on seeing both Bhim and Binod. "Ah, come inside my son! How have you been? And how come both of you are together?"

Binod bowed to Prasad and said, "Uncle, there is something very important that we need to discuss."

They went inside and Binod poured everything on what had happened in the past few days. With a very sorry face, he said, "I am so sorry. It is because of me that the trouble has come to us so soon. Else, we would have had much more time to look at other options. It is all my doing."

Prasad sank in his chair. He was not sure what to say. It was a difficult time. He had already seen a lot of violence and he knew for sure that more lay ahead. What was God punishing them for? Despite his best efforts, a small drop of tear trickled down from his eyes. Rakesh hugged his father. Binod and Bhim also came nearer.

Binod almost cried, "I am so sorry uncle. I know there is nothing that we can do now. We will have to face whatever comes. That's why I also have come to be with you all."

"This is not your fault, Binod. It was anyway something that we had to prepare against, only that we may not have much time now. But some day or the other, it was bound to happen. I am worried. Now you have also got involved. It will put you and your family also under threat," said a worried Prasad carefully wiping the tiny drops from the corner of his eyes. "Bhim, please bring some snacks from the market. Binod, have some food and then you go home immediately. It is important that you stay with your family and ensure that they are safe."

Bhim left to bring snacks from the market. He came back running in ten minutes. "Binod, Binod!" he was shouting from the main door itself. He ran inside the room where they were seated. He was sweating all over. He wanted to speak but was hesitating. His lips were quivering, his body shaking.

"What happened, dada?" asked a worried Binod. Others also stood up not sure what to expect.

"The guy…you know…the one who planted the bomb inside the restaurant…someone tried to kill him. Someone tried to hit him with a dagger. It aimed at his heart. Luckily, he ducked it and the dagger lodged in his arm. Fortunately, he managed to escape somehow. The dagger also appeared special – it had an eye crafted on it."

With the last piece of information, Binod, Rakesh and Prasad were convinced that it had to be the handiwork of Vikram. No one said anything. They just prayed in their heart for some miracle that would help them.

"Rakesh, I need to go home. I will contact you in the evening," said Binod. His mind was working fast trying to think what could be done in the situation. He hurriedly caught a rickshaw and went to his home.

❀ ❀ ❀

Chapter 44
Rakesh and Shakti get Summoned

"What are you saying? Are you out of your mind? You are just a student. Snooping around and getting involved with such dangerous criminals can get us all killed! You should have talked with me before taking such a step," Binod's father shouted at Binod hearing what all he had done. His whole family was worried. So far, they were completely untouched by the recent events although they were concerned about what was happening. But they were still far away and safe. But what Binod had done out of his love for his friends, had put them in grave danger.

Binod freshened up and went to rest in his room. He had not slept for last two nights and his mind was tired with all that had happened in the last few days. All his efforts had gone waste, in fact, they had back fired. Amidst these thoughts, he dozed off on his bed.

Just moments later, he was woken up with his father shouting at him, "Binod, the grocery store boy says that there is a call for you. Please don't go anywhere else. Just pick up the phone and come home after your conversation. Come soon." Binod did not have a phone at his home. It was normal for people to reach his family through the grocery store which had a phone. It was still not late in the evening. There was still sufficient day light outside. His father didn't expect any danger.

"It's Binod here," said a worried Binod not sure of what was coming up.

"Binod, Nirmala has been abducted again and taken to Bardah. One of the policemen had come here to say that. He is still stationed at the house for our safety," Bhim said in a low tone. Binod could sense that probably, Bhim had been sobbing.

"Where is Rakesh? Ask him to wait for me. I am coming straight away." Binod kept down the receiver. He said to the boy in the grocery store, "Please tell my family that I am going out and will return in a few hours. I am in a hurry." Even without waiting for a response, he caught the rickshaw outside the shop and asked him to speed away.

The fifteen-minute ride to Rakesh's house seemed like the longest he had ever taken. He was sweating despite a pleasant weather. He was extra attentive of his surroundings and if anyone got closer to the rickshaw, he was riding on his eyes would widen in anticipation of some danger. He handed a twenty rupee note to the rickshaw puller and jumped off even before it actually stopped near Rakesh's house. He ran inside. Shakti was also there. Even before anyone could say anything, there was a mild explosion outside. The policeman ran to see what had happened.

As soon as he ran out of the house, a jeep pulled outside Rakesh's house. Three muscular men jumped out of the jeep and came inside. Their demeanor said clearly that they were not friendly. One of them said in a coarse tone, "Rakesh and Shakti, come with us immediately". The tone was clearly meant to be an order rather than a request. There was no doubt in anyone's mind. It took them some time to digest what was going on.

Prasad was the one to speak first, "Who are you all and what is this about?"

The person said, "Vikram has asked for both. Don't waste your time or energy. No harm would be done. But if you don't come along right away, then there would be consequences." Both Rakesh and Shakti started standing up. Even Prasad had understood that if they meant any harm, it would have been done by now. There was no need to ask. There was no other way but to comply and hope for the best.

As Rakesh and Shakti walked to them, Binod also joined. He was already feeling guilty that his plans earlier had back fired. Angry, mostly against himself, he said, "They won't go anywhere unless I also come. My name is Binod, I am their friend."

The three gangsters did not know about Binod and the place they were coming from, they felt there was no need to know about such insignificant weak people anyway. They glanced at each other and nodded in affirmative, "Just don't try to play any trick. We really don't want any bloodshed." In just one sentence, they had tried to make them comfortable while making very clear the consequences otherwise.

They quickly climbed the jeep with the three friends- Rakesh, Shakti and Binod, and the jeep left off in speed. No one spoke for a long time. Lots of questions were flashing in the minds of the three friends. Vikram had not tried to harm any of them, unlike earlier instances. Nirmala had also been abducted earlier. Would they be going to the same place where Nirmala was kept? Why did Vikram summon them when he only wanted to know more about the crystal eye from Nirmala? Did he expect them also to throw light on it? The policeman back at Rakesh's house had been distracted by the explosion. Would he come to Bardah with more police force for rescuing them? Or had Vikram managed to bribe the policemen against such an eventuality? Would this be the last few hours of their life on this earth? Finally, Rakesh said clearing his throat, "Are we going to Bardah?" There was no response, but he already knew the answer. On one hand, he was worried as to what lay ahead. Would they be any match for the criminals there? There were so many of them, all armed with deadly arms. On the other, he was happy that he would be near Nirmala. He just prayed that she was alright.

Chapter 45
Vikram opens up

The jeep stopped just in front of Vikram's house. Rakesh had already been there. There was no change that he could spot. As soon as they entered, few more people came on their side. They were really scared. There was no way they could escape from so many people. But the good thing was that they were not harmed in any way so far. They were taken to a room on the first floor. Rakesh immediately recognized the room. It was the same where Nirmala was held the last time.

And before he could think more, he saw Nirmala sitting there. He looked carefully and could not believe his eyes. She was just sitting, there was no handcuff, no rope tied around her, absolutely nothing. Opposite her, there was the familiar face of Vikram sitting on another chair. As soon as they entered the room, the other men left the room and Vikram bolted the room from inside. Before closing, he gave some instruction to his men which no one could hear. Probably, he didn't want anyone to disturb them for some time.

He then signaled the three boys to sit on the chairs. He poured water from a jug into three glasses and gave it to them. "Have some water," he said. When he saw them hesitating, he said, "Don't worry, nothing has been added to the water. If that was my intention, you wouldn't be standing here anyway." He then turned towards Binod, "And who are you? I had just asked for Rakesh and Shakti."

Binod was glad that Vikram had not yet found out that he was the guy who tried to get him caught in the explosion at Calcutta. After a short pause, he said, "I am their friend. We all have grown together since childhood. I…"

"Look, I had asked only for Rakesh and Shakti. I don't know why they brought you here. If you want to leave, you may leave now.. I just have some questions that I want answers for from Nirmala. The only reason why I have brought these two also here is that I just didn't want any unnecessary disturbance from them. Probably my approach was wrong in the earlier instances. I have no enmity with any of you but there is something I am searching for and I guess Nirmala knows the answer."

They did not know what to say. Nirmala asked, "What exactly do you want to know? I really don't understand."

Vikram took a deep breath on hearing this and said, "Listen carefully. I want to share a story with you all. But first, I want you to see something." completing that sentence, he pulled up the sleeve of one of his arms and turned it towards them. All of them were surprised to see that Vikram also had an eye made on his arm. Nirmala's heart was pounding, "Was it some kind of trick that Vikram was trying to pull?"

As if Vikram read her thoughts, he said, "This is my birthmark, the same as that on Nirmala's arm. My father also had the same thing. I was born on the North Sentinel Island, far away from here." He then continued his story about how he and his mother reached Cooch Behar and then how his mother died in the political rioting in Calcutta.

"The boy whom I saved during the riot was Babloo, the one who died along with others in the burnt jeep when they were bringing Nirmala last year to Bardah." Vikram sighed. It was evident how much he loved Babloo. "Babloo's father was the don of Bardah. When he saw that I didn't have anyone left in this world, he adopted me as his own son. He loved me even more than Babloo. When his health started deteriorating, I had to take over his empire here. I didn't really like all these things - all this violence and other criminal activities. But then sometimes, fate enslaves you in myriad ways. I accepted it as my destiny. But I tried to reduce violence as much as possible. Since then, I also started helping the villagers. That is why they love us so much here now."

He continued, "What I am going to speak to you about is a secret and I don't want any of our discussion leaving this room. Of course, Nirmala already knows about it. You know this birthmark. There is a story prevalent on our island- a story which basically means that somewhere, there is a crystal eye, which has some magical power. It makes one immensely strong. Every child on our island grows with that story. Most take it as a fable. But when my mother was dying, she told me that story was correct. This means that indeed, there is a crystal eye somewhere which gives people super normal powers. I have been in quest of the same ever since. I had visited our island few years back to learn more about it."

❋ ❋ ❋

Chapter 46
The Flashback

Ever since Vikram settled with the Thakur family at Bardah, his miseries had gone away. He never had to sleep on an empty stomach. He never had to look out for pesky policemen trying to pin him down due to lack of proper documentation. Thakur had adopted him like a son. Thakur's men treated Vikram like Thakur's elder son. He soon got involved in the criminal activities of the family. He was always on the right side of law till he came to Bardah, but destiny turned in such a fashion that he could not say no to what was happening to him. He was slowly and steadily getting drawn into the criminal world of Thakur. He had sort of given up on life. He had already lost his loving father and the large extended family at the island. He and his mother had been running from one place to another ever since. And then he lost his mother too - the only true relationship that was all left for him since all that he lost during the Bhola cyclone. It is said that you never forget those with whom you have spent the worst days of your life. Similar was the bond that Vikram and his mother shared. It was unlike any other mother-son relationship. While he always enjoyed the love and care that his mother bestowed upon him, he never shied away from becoming a shield for his mother against anyone who tried to trouble her. This was despite his tender age.

And despite the comfort at Bardah, he never forgot any of the moments spent with his mother. Her last words still echoed in his ears – "The eye…the story of the crystal eye is real…go and find it…and take its blessings!"

By 1995, Thakur himself had been confined to a wheelchair. But instead of giving his so-called kingdom to his own blood, he chose the adopted elder son, Vikram, for leading it. Babloo, the younger son, also loved Vikram and there was no rivalry at all. Although Vikram had taken over the control, he didn't really like violence so much. He preferred to rule the hearts. He managed to convince the wheelchair-ridden Thakur and won over the villagers of Bardah. That turned Bardah almost into a fortress. It provided a lot of security to Thakur's family.

When Vikram was confident that he could take some leave, he went to Thakur, "Thakur ji, it has been almost twenty-five years since I left my hometown. Many a times, I dream of going there and finding out how people are. Now that things are stable here, I want to take a break and visit my folks for a few days."

Thakur thought for a while and nodded in affirmative. He even blessed Vikram as he touched his feet. Vikram did not tell him that more than his people, it was his mother's last words that he wanted to get more information on.

He took a flight from Calcutta to Port Blair. From there, he hired a small fishing trailer. He gave the owner sufficient amount so that he could drive the trailer himself. He remembered that when he earlier lived at the North Sentinel Island, their tribe never allowed any outsider to come to the island. In fact, they would even go to the extent of killing someone who would try to intrude. He wasn't sure then as to what it was that they were hiding or protecting from the world. He was not the four-year-old that had left with his mother in 1970. He was now almost twenty-nine, a grown-up man whom no one would recognize. He would only be seen as an outsider and there was a high chance that he could be killed before he could even say that he once belonged to that place.

As his trailer approached the shore of the island, he increased the speed of the trailer. As soon as the trailer was about to hit the ground, he shut its engine and allowed it to hit the shore. A shut engine would attract minimum damage and he would be able to leave on the same trailer after his work was done. He carefully jumped into the water from the side that was away from the shore. He lay under the water and waited to see if there was any movement anywhere. He crawled, lying down towards the shore and just lay there pretending to be unconscious. He had changed into a sleeveless shirt on the trailer earlier in the hope that someone would see the eye on his arm and spare his life.

As he lay on the ground, a small dart hit his leg. The dart did not cause a lot of pain and Vikram managed to keep still. Moments later, when his eyes opened, he found two tribal in front of him. His hand automatically went to check the wound of his leg. He was surprised to find a cloth tied on it and he felt from the smell as if some medicine had been applied over it.

"Ah, where am I?" he said in a low tone. He was not able to recognize any of the two tribal. They looked old but strong nonetheless.

"Who are you?" asked one of them, looking at his face and at his birthmark at times.

Vikram tried to look around and he was happy to see the same birthmark on one of them. "My name is Vikram. I was born on this island and had to leave it during a cyclone in 1970. My father was the leader of the tribe. His name was…"

Both tribal were surprised and looked at each other. "Shiv," said one of them surprised at the revelation. "Where have you been all these days? Your father had gone to save one of the men who had been washed over into the water. While saving him, he got a bite from a sea wasp. By the time Shiv could bring that man to the shore, he himself was unconscious. The cyclone was just about to hit. We saw him getting washed away into these waters. We tried but could not save him. I still remember…," he clenched his fist as his eyes became watery.

Vikram could see tears rolling down his cheeks. But the very next moment the tribal wiped his tears. "We tried searching for you and your mother. But we could not find you. In fact, most people had been washed away that day. We could not save most. Even after so many years, we are hardly 10-12 families left." He was staring into nowhere and appeared lost in his thoughts.

Then the other person said, "Where did you go that day? And what took you so long to return?"

Vikram then narrated his story. Hearing about the death of his mother, the one with the birthmark said, "Finally the cursed woman was relieved of her pain and misery," he joined his hands in prayer. He continued, "You obviously don't remember. My name is Bhura. Pawan and I were the two deputies Shiv had. What have you come here for now?" Since there were not many people left in the tribe, he gave instructions to the other tribal and sent him back inside the island.

Vikram said, "Bhura, I have a lot of questions. I am searching for their answers. Although my life has now turned more comfortable, I am not in peace with myself. You owe me answers for them. I don't intend to stay here. I have left this place once and for all. But I know for sure that I would find answer to my queries here only."

Bhura sighed. He knew what was coming. With almost nothing left in the island, he himself had thought at times to run away from the island and start a life afresh. But he had lost his family in the cyclone, a family he loved a lot. He had turned into a living dead anyway, just taking care of whatever families were left. "I am not sure what is it that you want to know, but let me see if I can be of any help. I owe this to the sincerity with which your father served the community as long as he was alive."

"First of all, why is it that you all called my mother cursed? Although I don't remember about my childhood days at the island much, I remember clearly that all gave a lot of respect to me and my father but ostracized my mother nonetheless. What was the reason for that?" asked Vikram.

"Vikram, my son. This is something that I will not be able to help you with. But rest assured that none of the men would ever do a thing like that unless it was the right thing to do. She had committed a grave crime and deviated from age old practices of the tribe. Probably that is why she lived a life of miseries. I won't be able to say more. But rest assured that no injustice was done to her."

Vikram was in a deep thought and he felt as if it was not right to push further. He said, "It would pain me forever Bhura. I wish I could do anything to remove the stain on her. But since you feel so strongly about it, I am not forcing you. There is only one more thing. I have learnt that the story of the crystal eye is not just a story. It is a true one. I want to know more about it."

Bhura's eyes were wide open on hearing this. His fists were clenched and eyebrows lifted in anger, "Who on earth told you this?"

Vikram could sense the uneasiness in Bhura's eyes. But he had come prepared that whatever it may be, he would not leave without finding the truth. Hesitatingly, he said, "Those were the last words of my mother."

"Ah, that wretched woman! She did it again! She was indeed cursed!" said an agitated and defeated Bhura. After few moments of cursing, he said, "Listen, I think I should share a bit more about your mother with you. You know, several years before your birth, three outsiders had been washed onto our island- two men and a woman. They were all unconscious. We killed both men, as is our custom. We were about to kill the woman too. But Shiv stopped us. He was drawn towards the woman. He requested us to spare her life. By that time, she gained her consciousness and started crying when she realized that she had lost the two brothers along with whom she had been washed ashore. Those were the only relationship she was left with in the world and with them gone, she was left all alone. She was hysterical. We took her to the elderly of the island to decide upon her fate. Shiv was adamant on not letting her die. Everyone respected Shiv since he had done a lot for the community. It was finally decided that only if Shiv married the woman, they would let her live. The woman also did not have anyone to go to. She quickly agreed to marry Shiv. However, few years later, she did something that we always feared for. That is the reason why we never allowed anyone inside the island. She told someone that the story of the crystal eye was true. As Shiv's wife, she deserved to know about it. But she was tied to the promise that she would never share it with anyone. She was not authorized. But she betrayed our trust. That is why everyone started distancing from her. And see, she told you as well! That cursed woman!"

Vikram was listening intently. At least, now it was confirmed that the story was true. He wanted to know more about it. But he didn't know if Bhura would tell him. Yet there was nothing else he could think of. Hesitatingly, he said, "Who was the person whom she told it about? What is the truth of the crystal eye? Please tell me more about it."

Bhura sighed. He looked at the sky for forgiveness. But he was not left with any other option. May be this is what the divine forces wanted. Reluctantly, he said, "Son, this is a very big secret. I can't tell you all about it. It is true that somewhere in the world, there is a crystal eye which has miraculous properties and can give magical powers. Somehow, our tribe was associated with how it came into being in the first place. But over the years, the exact location of the crystal eye has been lost. We really don't know if it is still at the same place where it was originally placed. In our tribe, not everyone is born with this birthmark, only a few who we believe are chosen by the God. Our leader, when he is about to reach forty years of age, then looks for his successor. He and his deputies look for three traits in all kids above ten years who have the birthmark." Bhura stopped there as if to take a break. He was after all an old man now.

"What traits, Bhura?"

"First, the kid should have the expertise of echolocate. You know that bats can't see. They send sound waves and from the echo, they learn about their surroundings. Some people can also imitate bats in same way. They can generate sounds and learn about their surroundings even with their eyes closed. The second is the ability to raise the temperature of their body without any external aid. You know, there is a special breathing technique which one can deploy while meditating about flames inside your body. That raises the temperature of your body significantly. Ages ago, several saints used to practice such techniques. It's a really difficult technique to master but can help you immensely against cold weather. The third is the one that we all were sure you already possessed, even in your early childhood. Unlike most humans, your body visibly showed much higher muscle concentration and reduced body fat. We were almost sure that you would be the heir to your father, Shiv," said a pensive Bhura.

Vikram now remembered that despite the fact that few other kids had the same birthmark, the tribal often came to take his blessings and not others despite the fact that he was just a small kid.

Bhura continued, "Shiv would have been proud to anoint you and handover the blessed bangle to you. That was the practice and then he would tell you whatever little information was left about the location. But destiny had other things in store for all of us. There are hardly few people left. I have been looking after them after Shiv's death. There are only two kids with that birthmark now. But they don't appear to have the three necessary traits. Perhaps the crystal eye story would just become another fable now." Bhura then stopped staring into nowhere again.

Vikram was surprised that Bhura tied with the promise of keeping the secret, had shared it with him, that too willingly, without much persuasion. Why? Whom had his mother shared the story with? And if Bhura cursed her so much for that, why was it that he shared the secrets?

But then, Vikram saw blood trickling down from Bhura's mouth. Bhura fell to the ground. Vikram was stunned, "What happened to you?"

Bhura said in a dying tone, "I know what you are thinking. Look Vikram, there is no one on the island now who could become an heir. I am pretty sure of that. Historically, it was never impossible to find an heir. But circumstances have changed dramatically. There are only two kids with the birthmark and I am pretty much convinced that they are not worthy enough. But I still want the story to live in this world. So, I have told you a lot." He was barely able to open his eyes. He raised his right hand and Vikram held it immediately. "I know I should not have broken my promise by telling you so much. But I have become selfish now. All these years, I have been desperate to see if we could have a legitimate heir. I have lost all hope. You have come like a silver lining. So I have told you whatever I could. I have not checked you for the presence of the three traits although I am confident that you already have the third one. I don't have much time left to check the other two. And even if you have, I am not sure if the tribe would accept you after such a long absence. So I have not told you anything about the location. I am taking a bet and pray…"

Those were the last words that came out of his mouth. Vikram let his hand rest on the ground. Near his hand, he saw a small ring like thing whose lid was open. He understood in a moment. "So, he poisoned himself so that he could not share whatever little he knew about the location with me. And his last bet was that if I am truly destined, then I would be able to locate the crystal eye myself."

An era had come to an end. Vikram had found the answers, quite a lot, even though some were missing. But he was sad that Bhura had to leave the world like this. "His death will not go in vain," He said, tears rolling down his cheek.

He pushed the trailer back into the water. He started the engine and left for Port Blair and then to Calcutta.

❀ ❀ ❀

Chapter 47

An Intruder Barges In

The four- Nirmala, Rakesh, Shakti and Binod were carefully listening to whatever Vikram was saying, word by word. Rakesh, then said, "So where does that fit us all in? And you said that you yourself disliked violence. But you tried to knock off my mother, Shakti's father, the attendant at my father's office. What are you saying?"

A surprised Vikram immediately said, "I know that is what anyone in your position would think. But trust me - I also don't know who had done any of this. I really don't. I wonder..."

Before he could say anything, the doors of the cupboard inside the room opened with a creaking sound. Everyone started looking towards it with alertness. They saw a frail looking man stumbling out of it. He was limping slightly and had he stood tall, he would have surpassed Vikram easily. He was bald and his eyes were big and black. His appearance itself was dominating. As he came out, he straightened himself a bit, tired by God knows how many hours spent inside the cupboard. He quickly raised both his hands above his head – a gesture that meant that he meant no harm to anyone.

"Well, if you guys allow me, Vikram is right that it wasn't him who had hit those people. It was me. And don't panic, I don't mean any harm to you all. But since we are trying to understand what all has happened so far, I thought of clearing out a couple of things, without which, the story may not be complete." He made himself comfortable on a chair next to Vikram. Vikram was also staring at him just like the other four in the room. Where had he seen him? His mind was trying but unable to place the intruder.

"My name is Mahesh," there was a pause and understanding that just the name did not make any sense, he added, "I am the elder brother of Vikram."

Vikram shot back, partly frustrated with the intrusion and partly surprised with the claim, "What are you talking about? I have never even heard of you? What is this all about?" His mind was still trying to place him. Where had he seen this lame man?

"I know. I don't share the legend like you. And our mother anyway made a mistake out of her love for me. And for the rest of her life, she was banished as the cursed one," said Mahesh.

Vikram remembered that Bhura did tell him that the reason why his mother was termed cursed was because she had talked about the truth of the crystal eye to someone. But he never mentioned that she told it to his own elder brother! "How am I supposed to believe this? You could easily be making up stories! It…"

Even before Vikram could complete his sentence, Mahesh said, "Listen, I think we all have gone through a lot and I am really tired. I just want it to end one way or the other. Let me share a few things and you only tell me if they are true or not. You did not kill the policeman that day at Cooch Behar. But he was found murdered. Who killed him? Did you hear anything unusual about that?"

Vikram suddenly remembered. A drunken policeman was trying to molest his mother at Cooch Behar one day. Vikram had hit him unconscious trying to save his mother. But then he heard while fleeing away from that place that someone had murdered him with a dagger, a dagger which had a crystal eye made on it.

He saw Mahesh taking out a similar dagger and putting it on the table near them. He had clearly not come to fight. Else he would not have kept it away on the table.

"Then at Calcutta, during the riot, how come so many people came to help you and your mother? Did you notice the lame man who kept the rioters away from you and your mother? Try to remember. Wasn't it me?" added Mahesh.

Binod looked at the dagger on the table without getting up. He said slowly, "And you are the one who killed the guy who set up the bomb at Sea Lounge!"

Vikram was confused at all that was going. He said, "If you are my brother, then why did you remain away for so many years?"

Mahesh said, with somewhat watery eyes, "Dear Vikram. I was born with a slightly weak leg. Now when I think of what the people on that island have been going through all these ages, my heart goes out for them. After living in this so-called outside world, I realized that how underprivileged those folks were. Had I been vaccinated, probably I would not have developed this in my leg. And I was not even born with the pride of the tribe - the birthmark of the crystal eye. But you know, our mother was also an outsider in the sense that she was not born in the tribe. So, her love for her crippled kid was much more than that for some tribe that she had married into. She pressed our father several times to share the secret and help my condition. But our father would never relent. One day, she saw some kids laughing at me when I fell down. She was very angry and with tears in her eyes, she let out the secret. She told me that the story was indeed true. Kids in our tribe were anyway independent much before their age. She told me to go out and look for it. The crystal eye would not only strengthen my leg but would give unparalleled powers to me. Somehow, Bhura heard this. And that's how she began to be called the cursed one. Unable to bear what I had brought upon her; I left the island one day and reached Andaman. I also took the ancient scripture which probably had some clue about the location of the crystal eye. From there, I reached Calcutta. Life is never easy for a cripple. It was really tough to make a living. That is when I turned to crime- from small snatchings in the beginning to feed myself, to robbery, illegal arms trade and murders and what not. But all this while, I had not found the crystal eye. I set one of my persons in Andaman to keep an eye on anyone who would ever come from the island. I didn't want to return and create more problems for our mother. But then I heard that the Bhola cyclone had destroyed everything. I got to know that you and mother had left from there. I was both happy and worried. I found out soon from my network that you both were at Cooch Behar. I wanted to actually bring you both with me. But I myself was leading a dangerous life, always trying to escape from death. I didn't want to expose you both to more danger. But that day when I heard about the policeman trying to molest our mother, you had already beaten him into unconsciousness by the time I reached. But I didn't want him to live. I knew he would create more trouble. So, I killed him with a similar dagger. And yes, that guy is right. I think someone had set you up at Sea Lounge along with Kim. I learned about it later and punished that guy. I think..."

Binod quickly said, "Well, now that all truth is coming out, let me fill that piece of puzzle for you. I knew that Vikram had lots of sympathizers in police as well as in politicians. So, it was difficult to frame him. But what if he was caught in the full glare of the media? Then probably it would be difficult for the police to let him go. This was the plan. But unfortunately, Vikram escaped."

Nirmala was stunned at all that was going on. Unable to take it more, she said, "But I am still not sure as to where do I fit in all this?"

Vikram quickly said, "Well, when I returned to Calcutta from the island hearing all from Bhura, I spent a couple of days there. One night when I was tired and sleeping in my room, I felt as if I was about to fall unconscious. My head was spinning. I slept that night like a baby but when I woke up in the morning, I realized that I had seen a dream. Bhura had only told me that the story was indeed true and it may just be possible that someone somewhere knew about the location. In the dream, I saw that in Munger itself, there was a girl who knew about the location. Her name was Nirmala. That is…"

Before he could complete, Mahesh said, "My apologies once again for interrupting here. Actually, that was not actually a dream but I had induced it upon you. It was my doing. Look, I have always been on the lookout for the crystal eye because I wanted to get rid of my physical limitations. So, I had been trying to find about it since long on my own. It is a long story actually."

❀ ❀ ❀

Chapter 48
Mahesh's Long Story

Mahesh realized that his physical limitations posed a big threat in his profession. He had been trying to find about the crystal eye since long. He was not sure of where exactly to search for. He had looked at the scripture that he had stolen from the Island. But the image did not make any sense.

He thought that there was a good chance that may be one of the ancient scriptures might have some information on it. He knew that most ancient travelers had documented a lot about unique things in India. In fact, even the kings at times had hired writers to pen down the riches of their kingdoms. He knew that not all things had been documented. Lots had been lost also. But he could not think of any better way to unravel the mystery. He learned that Nalanda was the most ancient seat of learning. In ancient ages, it was the largest university in the world. It had a huge library where thousands and thousands of ancient scriptures were kept. In fact, when Bakhtiyar Khilji burnt it in 1193, there were an estimated nine million books there. It is said that it took several months for the fire to be doused. Several manuscripts were lost but several still managed to see the light of the day.

Ages ago, Attila had to take Arya-Siddhanta hostage in order to learn more about the copper plate. But times had changed. Greed was everywhere and money had gained the sweetest melody ever. Mahesh bribed one of the scholars there and the scholar started to search for him. A digitization drive was already underway. So, whatever was already covered, it was pretty easy to check for. But they could not find anything which even remotely mentioned a crystal eye with magical powers.

After a few days, the scholar said, "There are a few even more secret manuscripts and artifacts from the Garbha, a supposedly hidden room inside the erstwhile library. But it is difficult to get access to that part. We will need to…"

Even before he completed his sentence, Mahesh knew what exactly the scholar was aiming for. Mahesh did not have much time. He said, "Take me there. I will give you a million rupees even if we don't find anything."

And that was all that the scholar needed to remove whatever were the bottlenecks in reaching those secret manuscripts and artifacts.

So far, Mahesh had not shown the ancient scripture that he had in his possession. "Maybe, after I take a look inside…," thought Mahesh.

The next day, the scholar took him to a large room which had cameras fitted all over. The room was locked with a biometric machine. "Don't worry, there is some problem with the electric supply here and it is likely to remain like that for another two hours. I am afraid that is all that we have for the time being. Hopefully, we would be able to complete our search by then."

Mahesh was not so sure. But he didn't have much of a choice. As they went inside, they saw that the room had a glass ceiling and it was lit by the light coming from the sun from above. In the center of the room, a very large pot like structure was kept with a peculiar neck. The scholar was looking around at various manuscripts. Several large palimpsests were kept. Few of them were so large that they had been rolled up.

But the pot had caught the attention of Mahesh. It was slightly smaller than him. It had a dark coating all over its body. There were two vertical lines running diametrically opposite each other from the neck. The neck itself was of eighteen inches. On the body, there was a small metal plate. It had a few lines scribbled on it. However, it was in Sanskrit and Mahesh didn't know to read it. He quickly called the scholar, "First tell me about this one. What is written on it?"

The scholar read it, "It is written in Sanskrit. It says that there is an ancient secret hidden in this pot. The pot carries Aryabhat's name. So probably, he is the one who created this one. It was a common practice to hide secrets in such a way that only a learned person could ever open it. These lines say the same thing. They say that they are locked by Aryabhat's name. There is a particular way to open it. If anyone tries to force it open, it would destroy the content inside." He hesitatingly added, "Look my friend, the electricity would be out for only thirty minutes more. We need to complete our search fast."

Mahesh kept staring at the metallic pot, "You are sure that there is nothing more written on the scrap? I mean, could there be a hint or something?" The scholar nodded in disagreement.

Mahesh said, "Ok, let us go out." The scholar was relieved to finish this mission. He didn't want anyone to catch him. Of course, the lure of money was there, but he didn't want to land up in prison. He was happy that he would get a million rupees for such a small work.

Mahesh had memorized each and every detail about the pot. He went back to rest in the night and kept thinking. What would be the purpose of the glass plate on the top? He had already sensed that the coating was some kind of explosive material. So, it was obvious that if someone tried to open it, any heat produced could explode the pot along with its contents. But what if someone poured water over it and then tried to cut through the pot keeping it cold simultaneously? But he knew that Aryabhat was not a fool. He was in fact one of the brightest minds that the country had ever produced. He could have mixed potassium or something else which could create an exothermic reaction when mixed with water. The heat would then do the same thing – explode the pot along with its contents.

He kept thinking about what more did he see. There were two vertical lines running diametrically opposite from the neck. These had coating different from the body of the pot but also smelled like some explosive. He didn't know why two different kinds of explosives were used. Could their strength be different? He had seen in movies how at times a thin line of explosive was used in order to open up hidden chambers or doors. It could fairly well be the purpose here too. If it was of a low intensity, then it won't really ignite the rest of the coating all over the pot. But why were they ending inside the neck? Was there some mechanism to actuate them from inside? What if someone tried to ignite only the two without using the mechanism inside the neck? Would it also ignite the other explosive? He wasn't sure. He slept thinking about the pot the whole night.

The next day, Mahesh said to the scholar showing a piece of paper, "Dear friend. This is the confirmation for your money transfer. Thanks for taking me to that place. But you know that our work isn't really finished. I need more time there. I need to see that place for another two hours. If you can arrange it today, I can give you another half-a-million rupee."

The scholar had grown greedy, "But it is very dangerous. You know how I had to cut the electricity in order for the cameras and other security to be shut. If we keep doing so, it may arouse suspicion. We might get caught. No my friend, this is really difficult now. I think I am done with helping you. We must part our ways now." But inside his mind, he was really hoping for a better bargain.

And Mahesh had already read his mind. "Alright, I will wire another million. But that is all I am left with now. Prepare for the same tomorrow," said an agitated Mahesh. He was angry that it had been quite long time he had spent there without any success. He had also given around half-a-million in cash to the scholar while the rest he had mentioned that he had wired. But Mahesh was himself a hardcore criminal. He knew that as soon his work was done; he would not need the scholar. The proofs he had shared of the money transferred were all fake. In fact, he had planned to kill the scholar once the work was done. He smiled to himself and left from the place. The scholar was smiling because he thought he was about to get loads of money again the next day.

"Come, I have shut the electric supply again," said the scholar as they entered the place where the pot was kept. Mahesh carefully saw the neck and the two vertical lines. He was sure that the explosive in the lines was of a much lesser intensity and that if they ignited leaving the rest of the pot untouched, then the pot would split into two parts and the contents would be safe. But if he tried to either force cut the metal or even pour water over it while cutting, then the pot would explode. His mind was racing against time to find some solution. "If it has to be explosive, then heating is the only solution. There is no doubt. But then the heating mechanism is inside the neck." He carefully looked at the glass on top of the pot. It was a thick glass and there were certain lines made over it.

"The Garbha where these materials were kept also had a similar ceiling. There also, the pot was kept at the center and the glass was staring into the sky," said the scholar. That sentence stayed with Mahesh. He carefully looked at the glass ceiling from which sunlight was coming. What if one could use the sunlight coming from the top to create heat inside the neck sufficient enough to ignite the explosive lines? That was entirely possible. But he didn't want to test a loose hypothesis. He again looked at the lines on the glass. What were they trying to tell? The glass was thick. So, if someone tried to remove it, definitely the sunlight passing through it could be channelized through a lens in order to create sufficient heat for the ignition. But the lines on the glass did not make any sense. Something in his mind told him that there was some trick there. What if he broke the glass and the whole pot ignited? He would not be able to see the content inside. He tried to see if he had missed anything. Half an hour had already passed away. As he moved around the pot, his eyes got stuck on Aryabhat's name written on the neck. It was not written in consistent thickness. There was something peculiar about it. Some parts of the name were much bolder than the other. He took out a small paper from his pocket and randomly drew only the parts which were written in bold. He carefully looked at it for some time and then smiled at his brilliance. He then wrote the word "Om" in Hindi on another piece of paper. Then he carefully struck each part one by one that he had randomly drawn on the earlier piece of paper. Bingo! The bold part of Aryabhat's name when combined together, formed a perfect "Om"!

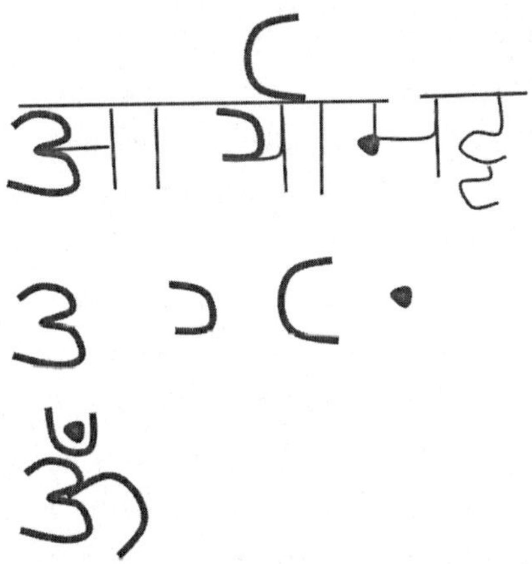

Mahesh knew exactly what to do now. He stood in front of the pot on the side where the scrap metal was attached. Obviously, this was the front part of the pot. He took his pen and marked the lines on the glass such that an "Om" was formed. He then carefully took out a bottle from his pocket. He carefully poured the liquid on the "Om" that he had written. There was little vapor around as the glass melted at those lines in order to create an empty space which resembled an "Om". It was already noon and there was a lot of sunlight coming from the top. He pulled the scholar from the pot. Within just next few minutes, a burnt smell started to fill the room. The sunlight from the ceiling falling through the *Om* had ignited something inside. With few sparkles, they saw the two lines on the outside of the pot being ignited. The scholar was horrified, "What are you…"

Mahesh shut his mouth. His eyes were red and the scholar took it as a command. The very next moment, as the two lines ignited completely, the pot split into two symmetrical halves. Mahesh saw a copper plate inside. He carefully looked if there could be any other traps. Confirmed that there were none, he took the copper plate, pulled the scholar near and ordered him to take him out. Mahesh knew that he could not leave the scholar yet. He could be of help in getting to a safer place. They carefully left the room and then the premises. As soon as they were out, the scholar gained strength to argue, "What the hell did you just do? You have broken an antique pot which had a secret! And why have you stolen that? You could just see that and leave it there. These ancient things are no less than invaluable treasures! You have put me in trouble. There would be police all over the place in no time!"

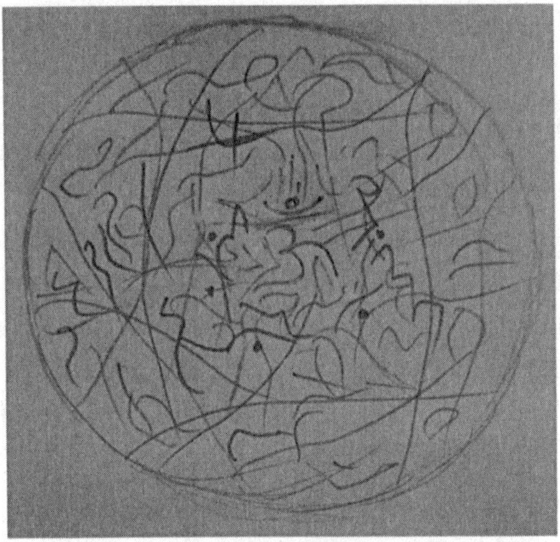

But Mahesh was already done with his quest and the scholar too. He didn't want to waste any more time. He saw that there was no one around. He pushed the scholar without saying anything. A helpless scholar tried to run after him. But a dagger pierced through his heart stopping him in his stride. He fell down immediately. Mahesh walked away without even looking back. The dagger was no common one. It had an eye crafted over it.

Mahesh was still not sure if the copper plate was connected in any way to his quest. But he had already seen the rest of Nalanda and he had not found anything else. He went to his room and carefully looked at the copper plate. It had a temple like outline made over it. There was a statue of Chandi made over it. There was a Shivalinga made outside the boundary of the temple. It was a strange Shivalinga. It had an ornate wheel crafted on it with seven spokes. Each spoke had an eye made over it, the same that he had seen on his father's arm, the same that featured in the crystal eye story, the same that his mother said was true, not just a mythological story! He looked carefully at the copper plate again. Above the wheel, a crystal eye was also crafted. The artist had drawn few rays emanating out of it. There were few numbers written on it- 26.5110°N, 84.6884°E. He quickly realized that these were longitude and latitude of a place.

The next day, he searched for the co-ordinates. It was of a temple named Chandi Asthan in a city named Munger- a small and quiet town on the banks of river Ganges. Had he finally reached his destination? Did it depict the location of the crystal eye that he was looking for? Or did it refer to something else?

Mahesh wanted to be more certain. He then took out the scripture that he had stolen from the island. He looked carefully at it to see if there was any way to link it to Munger.

He was always perplexed by the asymmetry of the image. The right eyebrow was slightly higher than the left one. He understood that it was difficult to draw during ancient ages. But despite limited tools, whatever ancient images he had seen at temples, were all beautifully created. Was it done deliberately? It wasn't only the asymmetry of the eyes which caught attention. One ear had an ornament while the other one didn't! There was only one hand made which appeared to carry a mountain but there were two small lines made on the mountain. He remembered how he had shown it to few historians but none could make out anything. He knew that perhaps archaeologists could understand it better. But he had hesitated to refer to them. It would certainly make them suspicious and he didn't want to lose the eye at any cost. But now that he had probably found another clue, he was set to up the ante.

He was repenting as to why he killed the scholar who had helped him in getting the copper plate. "Perhaps, he could have helped in unraveling the mystery! But aren't there others who could help? Is it worth taking the risk?"

The next day, he approached the vice-chancellor of the modern-day Nalanda University. This was set-up just next to the ancient ruins in order to revive the glory of the erstwhile university. He had changed his appearance in order to avoid even the remotest chance of being identified.

Mahesh said, "Madam, my ancestors belong to this city. But due to some reasons, we had to migrate to Kolkata decades back. It was the wish of my great-grandfather to contribute towards rebuilding of the university. Unfortunately, we were not so well off. However, God has been very kind since past few years and our business has soared to new heights. Since your university is trying to revive the ancient learning methodologies, we want to contribute something towards your organization. If you kindly allow me, I would like to donate a sum of ten million rupees."

A wide smile adorned the face of the vice chancellor. After all, the university was still under construction. The funds from the government were always sparse and late. This generous aid would certainly help her tide the current financial stress. She said, "I am so touched to see the devotion that your family has towards this ancient city. Several people come, visit, take photographs and just leave the place. The ruins have so far been neglected. Government has been trying to preserve whatever it can. Although our university has not yet been completed, we have started several courses and there are many scholars working on digitization of the scriptures etc. However, we are a government organization. It becomes difficult to accept large donations from individuals. I will have to explain to authorities…"

Even before she could complete, Mahesh interrupted, "Madam, I fully understand your predicament. But I don't have much time. I am here only till tomorrow. Talking to the authorities would take a long time. May I propose something? I have an interesting image which has been passed on in our family since ages. None of us know what exactly it depicts. That knowledge has been lost somehow. What has remained is just the commitment to keep it safe across generations. Is it possible to organize a contest among your scholars to decode the same? The one who succeeds can keep a part of the prize money while the rest can go entirely to your organization.

But since it is my ancestral property, I would take away the same once the competition is over."

The vice chancellor nodded in agreement. However, she looked a bit concerned. Mahesh read her mind, "Even if no one succeeds, you can keep the prize money for their efforts. For me, it is just a way to expedite things." He saw smile returning to her face.

He quickly left her office. He got an image of the scripture made on a large paper. He returned with that copy to the vice chancellor.

Out of ten million, Mahesh kept one lakh for the one who would win the competition. It was a huge sum for poor scholars working on government stipends. The next day, twelve scholars assembled. Some had experience in epigraphy while others had studied numismatics. They were already involved in studying the ancient scriptures kept at the ancient monument and deciphering & digitizing them. Mahesh announced a deadline of two days for deciphering the copy. It was kept in a large hall. The scholars were to work in the same hall. They were free to bring whatever books and tools they wanted.

Mahesh was keenly watching them work. The vice chancellor had left after the initial remarks. She had other work to do, while for Mahesh, it was of greatest importance. He saw the competitors drawing and redrawing the scripture in different ways in their notebooks. They were trying to slice it in different angles and rejoining few parts in order to check if they could decipher anything. By the end of the day, they were still scratching their heads and struggling with the assignment.

"Do we have any progress here?" asked a worried vice chancellor looking at the scholars still working hard at it. It was almost eight in the night by then. She was worried of losing the ten million. It would help her immensely in paying salaries to her staff which was witnessing delay from the government. She prayed for some miracle.

Looking at her body language, Mahesh understood that it was going to be difficult. He said, "Madam, this is just a small competition. The purpose only is to fulfill the desire of my great-grandfather. May I suggest something? Why don't we divide these guys into two teams? May be if they worked together, they could try out different perspectives and solve it? What do you suggest?"

The vice chancellor said, "Indeed! It is a really good idea!"

Mahesh then gathered all the competitors and announced that vice chancellor would form two teams of six people each. He also announced that he would raise the prize money to six lakhs instead of one lakh. Vice chancellor was more than grateful. She quickly divided the teams. Mahesh and the vice chancellor left the hall.

The scholars also left the hall for dinner. Instead of calling it a day, both teams returned in full strength and kept working on the image. Mahesh returned to his hotel. But he could also not sleep. It was a tense night. In the hall, the two teams kept working throughout- looking into several books and discussing among themselves. They were not novices. Each had done extensive study of ancient scriptures, history and culture. But the problem was that the image could belong to any era. Scripts have seen continuous transformation in India. At times, ancient scriptures were influenced by foreign culture and language like Greek, Persian, Arabic and what not. In fact, sometimes, people ascribed unnecessary importance to ancient images while most of them were just scribbling or devoid of any significant meaning. What if the image in front of them was just one of those- devoid of any significant meaning, or just a small attempt of say, a kid's drawing!

The bright sunlight woke up a tired Mahesh. His eyes were swollen. He had not been able to sleep last night thinking about whether the teams would be able to succeed. He quickly looked at the wall clock. It was half past seven in the morning! He quickly dressed up, had a quick breakfast and changed his appearance back to the one he had adorned yesterday. By the time he dashed to the hall, he was surprised to see only few people in the hall. Out of them also, two were sleeping on a bed-sheet on the ground while one was sleeping on the desk. As soon as they heard footsteps, they sprang to their feet. Mahesh could not make out much from their tired postures. They looked like college students working on some project over-night. As he approached them, he saw one of them approaching him with excitement.

"Good morning sir! I think we have finally solved it!"

Mahesh could not believe what he was hearing. "Are you sure? I mean, what exactly does the picture suggest?"

"Sir, this is an ancient image. If you would know, we currently use Devanagiri script for writing. But this was a much later development. The earliest of the scripts in ancient India was Brahmi. All other scripts sort of evolved from it slowly and steadily."

He then brought a couple of papers with full of sketches and rough notes. He continued, "Look at the eyebrows and the lines making the nose. Do you notice that these are asymmetrical?"

Mahesh nodded. He was always perplexed by this asymmetry.

"This is basically a Brahmi word- *Ma*. The two eyebrows make it *Mo*. Then, you would also notice that there is only one hand. If you look carefully, it signifies another alphabet- *Da*. Then there is a mountain that you see on the hand. If you look carefully, there are two small lines at the top of the mountain- ne horizontal and the other vertical. That is the alphabet- *Gi*."

Then another scholar added, "The last one was the trickiest. You see that ornament in the right ear. That is actually an inverted alphabet- *Ri*."

An anxious Mahesh could not hide his excitement. "So, what does all this mean? We have four alphabets- *Mo Da Gi* and *Ri*? Where does it take us now?"

The first scholar then continued, "You have already decoded it, sir. You combine the alphabets in the order that you just spoke and you get not one word but two- *Moda Giri*. It is the name of an ancient town of Bihar- Munger. An ancient copper plate dating back to eighth century, commonly known as the Devapal's copper plate of Munger, mentions the name of the place as *Moda Giri*. The image refers to the same place."

Mahesh was now happy. The image also mentioned the same place that was mentioned by the relic found in Aryabhata's mysterious glass chamber. "Munger it is then!" he mumbled softly, his eyes wide open with excitement.

By the time, the vice chancellor had also arrived. She was beaming with pride that her scholars had been successful in decoding the image. She clapped in excitement.

Mahesh followed the vice chancellor to her office and immediately wired the amount from his mobile to the university's bank account. He also wired the amount that was to be distributed among the team members that had deciphered the image.

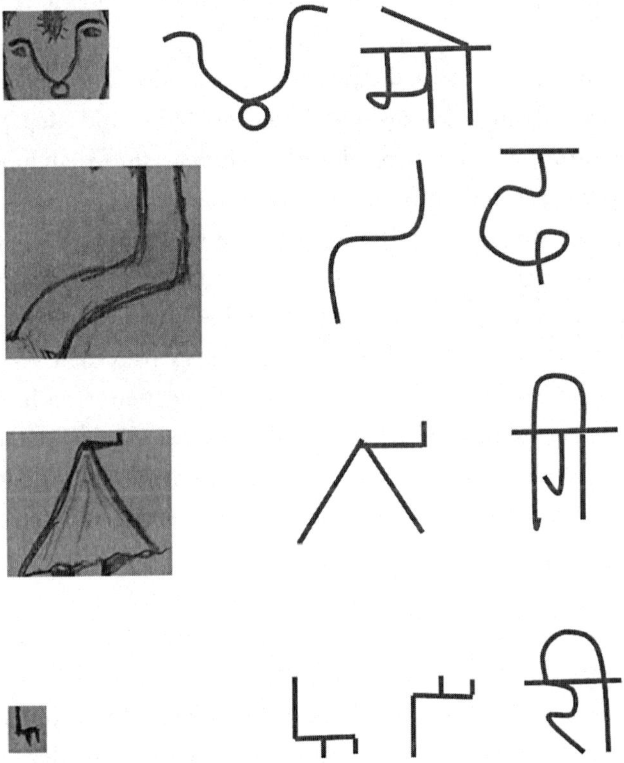

At last, the crystal eye was to be his. He slept what appeared to him in deepest and most comfortable sleep for God knows how many years!

He quickly left for the city. He was happy that years of search would now be over. He would seek the blessings of the crystal eye and would be cured of his physical limitations. He would not be a cripple any more. Would it also impart him magical powers? The story of the crystal eye that he had heard millions of times at the island mentioned exactly the same – that the prince had acquired supernatural strength from the eye. With that, he was able to defeat the demon who had single handedly defeated his father and king and his army and imprisoned them. He was sure that unless there was some truth, the tribe would not cast his mother as cursed. The story had to be true. He would also defeat his opponents and rule the world!

As soon as he reached the city, he reached the Chandi Asthan temple. He had left the copper plate back in his room. But he remembered every single detail mentioned on it. He was amazed to see that the boundary was exactly like the one on the plate. There was a long queue at the temple. He was eager to check if the deity was also the same as crafted on the copper plate. "Wait for your chance, my son. What is the hurry? You must have patience in a holy place," said the old lady ahead of him as his foot touched her. Mahesh quickly apologized. It took almost an hour for his chance to be face-to-face with the statue of the deity and it seemed like the longest wait of his life. As soon as he saw the deity, his eyes filled with tears of joy. It was the same as that on the copper plate! He started shivering in nervousness. After all, he would soon get the crystal eye and he was feeling nervous to finally get what he had been searching for the whole of his life! He took the offering and came out of the temple. "So, the copper plate mentions this temple. But the Shivalinga has been shown outside the boundary," he said to himself. Just to make sure, he once again searched all statues inside the temple in case he could find the Shivalinga. But there was none. He then decided to look around. He found two crematoriums on either side of the temple. "Should I speak to the priest and try to find out about nearby temples," he asked himself.

Later, he asked for the priest of Chandi Asthan. The priest appeared busy with his chores. He went to the place where the priest was working. He saw a donation box near him. He started saying *gayatri mantra* in a loud voice. As soon as the priest turned towards him, he quickly took out few five hundred rupee notes and put them inside the donation box slowly enough for the priest to see. Which priest doesn't like rich devotees? Mahesh then moved towards the priest and said, "Baba, I seek your blessings. I hear that this is a very holy place and people come from far off places to visit it. I have also come from Calcutta. I was told by my friend that there are lots of temples around here. Please tell me about them so that I can spend my time judiciously here." Mahesh had his head bowed. Looking at his limp, the priest understood. After all, when people need something badly, that is when they remember God! Perhaps this devotee was also seeking freedom from his physical pain. He said, "Now that you have come here, I am sure that Goddess Chandi will bless you and your sufferings will be gone. There are lots of temples here. In fact, there are lots of famous places in Munger that people visit. But in this part of the city, this is the oldest and most sacred. There are lots of other smaller temples too. But all of them are much newer. There is one Ganesh temple about two hundred meters away. Then there is a Durga temple another half a kilometer away. There is a Shiv temple also near that. But these are all new ones only. If you have come here, I think it would be sufficient," said the old priest. He was also worried that if the person in front of him went to each and every temple, his condition would worsen instead of recovering.

"Many thanks, baba," a confused Mahesh left the priest. He then searched around Chandi Asthan for next few days. He went to every temple that he could find. Although he had the co-ordinates, he even tried to increase the radius of his search in case he could find the Shivalinga made on the copper plate. But to no avail. He was utterly frustrated. The crystal eye on the Shivalinga of the copper plate could not be a mere coincidence. He was sure of that. But he had not found anything yet. How could he search for it? He was not very sure.

As he was walking, he bumped into a lean and thin girl. He apologized immediately, "I am so sorry dear. I just could not see you." In fact, Mahesh himself had fallen onto the ground. The girl gave him her hand. Mahesh reluctantly took the same. He did not fail to notice that the girl had a strange bangle on her wrist. It had eyes made all over. He kept staring at it when the girl spoke, "Are you alright? This is just a bangle I bought from the fair last year, just a small piece of steel." Mahesh stood and came back to his senses, "I am so sorry. I just thought it was bit strange looking."

The girl replied again, "There are lots many available in those shops. If you want, you can buy it from one of the shops." Just then she turned around suddenly and ducked a piece of stone that some urchin had thrown. She immediately balanced herself and smiled at Mahesh.

Mahesh smiled and walked away. He didn't have any interest in bangles. He was more intent on the crystal eye. But in the meantime, he had a more pressing concern that needed his attention. He returned to Calcutta. The crystal eye could wait.

Chapter 49
Mahesh Goes to Andaman

"Are you sure?" asked a surprised Mahesh. It was 1995 and Mahesh had just learnt from one his men that Vikram had bought a ticket for Port Blair. Why would Vikram go to Port Blair? His operation did not stretch so far. Was he trying to return to the island for something? But that was dangerous and stupid. Even Vikram knew that no outsider was allowed to enter the island. As soon as anyone spotted him there, he would be killed. Well, there was only one way to know more about it.

Mahesh reached Port Blair. He found Vikram bargaining with a fisherman for hiring his trailer. That made Mahesh confident that Vikram was indeed trying to go to the island all by himself. Mahesh wanted to go with Vikram. But he knew that it was not possible. So, he hid a powerful microphone in the trailer. An unsuspecting Vikram did not expect anything like that. As soon as the trailer hit the shores of the island, Vikram jumped out and pretended to be lying hurt. Although Mahesh was not there, the scene was near enough for Mahesh to hear everything.

And Mahesh was stunned at what he heard Bhura saying - *"Shiv would have been proud to anoint you and handover the blessed bangle to you. That was the practice and then he would tell you whatever little information was left about the location."*

Didn't he come across a similar bangle at Munger some time back? But the girl had said that the bangle was just ordinary and that she had bought it from one of the shops. She had also said with confidence that he could purchase the same from the shops. Mahesh was feeling stupid! How could he expect her to tell him the truth about the bangle? In fact, if she knew that he was looking for the crystal eye, she would go to all length in order to hide her identity. Or was it all just a coincidence? Could it really be just another bangle? He pondered over everything that he could remember. His mind was pacing fast. He suddenly remembered that someone had hurled a stone in their direction and Nirmala had turned immediately and ducked itaway. Mahesh also remembered about the three necessary traits that Bhura had mentioned to Vikram. How did Nirmala duck the stone which came from behind? Was this the property of echolocate? He thought for some more time and by the end, he concluded that what Nirmala was wearing was not any ordinary bangle. It was indeed the blessed one. Nirmala was also an heir who possibly knew all about the crystal eye, including its location.

Soon Vikram reached Calcutta. He spent a few days there. One night, when he was very tired, he felt a bit dizzy. He returned to his room and dozed off. And then he dreamt about Nirmala...

Chapter 50
The Dream

Moments back…

One night, when Vikram was having his dinner at one of the restaurants in Calcutta, Mahesh bribed a waiter to slip a tablet inside his drink. The drink made him dizzy. Vikram started feeling uncomfortable. He was feeling tired. “Maybe a lot of travel in the hot and humid weather has taken a toll,” he thought. He quickly tipped the waiter and left for his hotel in a taxi. By the time he reached, he was not able to walk on his own. Taking support of the handle of the staircase, he slowly climbed up to the second floor where his room was located. He was not able to see clearly. An attendant, who saw him, thought that he might have been drunk. He offered to help and opened the door of his room for him.

Inside his room, he closed the door immediately and fell on the bed. He was almost unconscious, unaware of what was going around him but still able to hear things. Right then, Mahesh who was already waiting inside for Vikram, started playing a recorder repeatedly, “Vikram, the crystal eye is real. A girl in Munger named Nirmala wears the blessed bangle. She knows about the location of the crystal eye."

He played the recorder several times till he was sure that Vikram had fallen into deep sleep. He had hoped that in the morning, Vikram would remember those words as if they appeared in his dream. And that was exactly what had happened. The subconscious mind trapped what was being relayed continuously. Vikram woke up in the morning feeling as if he had dreamt about the next clue – Nirmala at Munger, who probably knew about the location of the crystal eye!

❁ ❁ ❁

Chapter 51

The Last Piece of the Puzzle

Finally, the pieces of the puzzle were fitting in. Vikram had returned to the island and had learned more about the crystal eye. But he was not aware of the location yet. Mahesh, who had also heard the whole conversation between Bhura and Vikram, had related how he had seen a girl with the blessed bangle – Nirmala at Munger. The location mentioned on the copper plate also was in Munger and this was more than a mere coincidence. He was sure that Nirmala knew about the location of the crystal eye. Then he managed to impregnate Vikram with the idea through a dream.

"But I still do not understand one thing," asked a confused Binod. "If you knew that Nirmala already had knowledge about the location of the crystal eye, why did you involve Vikram? You yourself have resources enough to confront her directly and learn about it!" The question was directed towards Mahesh.

Mahesh sighed. "True, I could have tried to forcefully get the answer from Nirmala. I also have a sufficiently large criminal network. But…"

Before he could say anything, he fell onto the ground. Droplets of blood could be seen trickling from the side of his lips. Vikram immediately went to help him sit back on the chair. He was wondering what had happened to him all of a sudden.

A tired looking Mahesh sat back in the chair. He said in broken words, "I could have done this myself. But I have become terribly sick since last two years. God has never been kind to me. I was born a cripple and then I was diagnosed with last stage cancer last year. That is why I have been trying to get hold of the crystal. I don't want to die. I have to regularly go for my medication. That's why it was not possible for me to pull this myself and I involved Vikram, my younger brother. Nirmala…please help me urgently. I can't take it anymore. I need the powers of the crystal eye, or else I will die."

Vikram was very confused. Nirmala said, "I really don't know what you guys have been talking about. There is some big misunderstanding somewhere. I really don't know anything about any crystal eye."

Mahesh shouted back,"I don't have much time. Don't try to me. I need to know now or I will shoot you all!" He stood with a sophisticated gun in his hand.

That was a worrying sight and Rakesh, Binod, Shakti and Nirmala stood up immediately and became alert. Vikram was still composed but very confused. He was now sure that Nirmala was aware of the location. Or she knew at least something about the location that he didn't.

Mahesh's condition was deteriorating. He was becoming nervous. "Look Nirmala, I promise that I will leave you all once you tell me about its location. Can't you see that I am dying? What have I done to deserve this suffering? Don't I have the right to live?" he almost shouted. The hand in which he was holding the gun was quivering. Vikram and the other four were scared of what would happen if the trigger went off by mistake. And their fear turned into reality the next moment.

Bang! Bang! Mahesh fired two shots in quick succession, not aimed at anyone in particular. It appeared that he was trying not to let go of the gun while his hands were losing the strength to hold on to it. Everyone looked at the direction in which it was pointed. One bullet had pierced Binod's stomach. He had fallen on the ground. Nirmala, Rakesh and Shakti quickly sat down to check on Binod. Vikram, who anyway did not like much violence, was stunned. He looked at Binod and then at Mahesh. He suddenly realized that Mahesh was lifting his gun again. As Mahesh fired the next shot, Vikram lunged ahead in front of Nirmala. The bullet missed her but lodged inside Vikram's leg. Hearing the bullet sounds, several of Vikram's men came running to the room. Finding that the room was bolted from inside, they broke open the door to find Binod and Vikram lying in blood on the ground and Mahesh, whom they had never seen, trying to sit on the chair with a sophisticated gun in his hand. They quickly understood that it was Mahesh who had hit Vikram. Even before Vikram could stop them, one of his men sprayed a volley of bullets on Mahesh, killing him instantly.

"No!" shouted Vikram, still lying on the ground. After all, he had never known that he had a real brother before. And after meeting him, he really wanted to straighten things up. He had no blood relationships left and he really wanted someone with whom he could share the joys and sorrows of his life. Even Thakur's son Babloo, who was like his younger brother, had been killed last year.

But who could control destiny? Mahesh was motionless now. Vikram crawled towards him. Binod was losing blood quickly. Rakesh, Shakti and Nirmala did not know what to do. The very next moment, they heard wailing sounds of police vans growing louder and louder.

Chapter 52
The Hospital Scene

As Binod opened his eyes, he saw his parents. Both were smiling although their eyes were full of tears. He tried to move his hand but realized that a drip bottle was attached to his arm. He looked around. He was in a hospital. He realized that he had been shot by Mahesh.

The doctor came in and said, "How are you feeling young man?" Without waiting for his reply, he checked Binod's pulses, his medical file and said to his parents, "He is a brave boy and has been doing pretty well. All parameters are normal. I think he would be able to leave the hospital in a day or two. But at home also, he needs to take ample rest for another fortnight before he can do any kind of hard work.

Binod's parents stood with folded hands in front of the doctor. He had saved Binod's life. Binod looked around anxiously. Binod's father understood. Clearing his throat, he said, "Wait, I will call your friends. They are outside." He went out and came along with Rakesh, Shakti and Nirmala. All of them were happy to see Binod. "How is the brave engineer doing?" asked Rakesh.

Binod said, “I am fine. What happened…?” He was unable to speak more. Shakti asked him to keep quiet and said, “Due to the blood loss, you fell unconscious and I know you are eager to know what happened post that.” He narrated the whole story in short.

Vikram had lunged forward and saved Nirmala from getting hurt when Mahesh had fired the third bullet. But the bullet lodged itself inside Vikram’s leg. Hearing the shots, Vikram’s men had come up and barged in the room after breaking the door. They quickly understood that Mahesh had tried to shoot Vikram and one of them killed Mahesh on the spot. Vikram wanted to save Mahesh but the person opened his fire even without listening to Vikram. Soon, three jeeps full of police arrived on the scene. As soon as the police came, they shot at Vikram. Vikram was already hurt in his leg. He could not take the second bullet and died. The police then brought Binod into the hospital and informed his parents.

Chapter 53
And the legend lives on

Rakesh, Shakti and Binod assembled at Kashtaharni Ghat after a few days when Binod got back on his feet. They moved to a lonely place overlooking the mast of Sita Charan temple. Binod sighed, smiled, and said, "Looks like the warning about the crystal eye was correct."

They all were remembering the adventure of Mir Qasim's Tunnel they had chanced upon the previous year. Although they were not any of the heirs like Vikram or Nirmala, through their brilliance, hard work and above all- sheer luck, they had come across the crystal eye – in fact not only the crystal eye, but the whole tunnel architecture and the purpose for which these were created. They felt blessed to have come so close to the ageless epic – the Ramayana. There was a small poem written on a jigsaw puzzle inside the temple that housed the Shivalinga with the crystal eye. The last paragraph had said:

The power is so profound
It will help someone who found
But only the righteous may strive
For others wouldn't survive

"Shakti, look who is here!" shouted Dubey ji, Shakti's father from a distance. Announcing the arrival of a stranger, Dubey ji left. As the three ran upstairs, draped in an azure plain *saree* was a lean and thin figure coming towards them slowly. The cool evening breeze appeared to be playing with a flock of hair on her left side. Her left arm was holding a part of her saree which was swaying gently with the wind, much more beautiful than the waves on the river Ganges. Rakesh's heart was throbbing hard. He suddenly started walking quickly and Shakti and Binod were left a little behind. As he approached, a smiling Nirmala stood in front of him, her right fist loosely holding the left wrist and dangling a bit nervously. She was still wearing the blessed bangle. Their eyes met but no one spoke. As people say, silence itself speaks a lot.

As Shakti and Binod caught up, they were delighted to see Nirmala there. Understanding that the situation was becoming embarrassing, Binod spoke, "Look who's here!"

Shakti said, "It is such a pleasure to see her highness!" He bowed down on his knees giving her a royal reception. That broke the spell in which Nirmala and Rakesh were bound. They sheepishly smiled. They were meeting almost after a fortnight after Binod was back from the hospital. He was still advised not to do any laborious work, but rest all was fine.

Nirmala spoke, "I have come along with my father. He is at Shakti's house. I just wanted to thank all of you guys for your efforts to save me. You all have gone through a lot in the past few days. I really am..."

Before she could complete her sentence, Binod said, "Don't thank us dear. We just tried to do whatever best we could. And we are really happy that it has ended." He then nudged Rakesh who was still staring at Nirmala and had not spoken a word. Rakesh realized suddenly and felt embarrassed.

Rakesh said, "It really does feel good to be over with the past. And..." He was struggling with words. Both Binod and Shakti understood well. Rakesh was face to face with the girl whom he had fallen in love with and straight away gone to war to save her, risking a many lives. They had not had the chance to meet and talk in circumstances where they could have learned more about each other. They were sure that Nirmala also understood that Rakesh was in love with her. And the way they could read, it did appear that Nirmala had also developed a soft corner for Rakesh, if not anything else.

And Rakesh didn't want Nirmala to be influenced by what he and his friends had done in the past few days. A relationship based on debt doesn't last for long. And he could wait till they knew each other better. For some reason, no one spoke about the crystal eye and its magical powers. Rakesh, Shakti and Binod were already aware of almost everything about it although Nirmala wasn't aware of their knowledge. The three friends didn't know to what extent Nirmala knew about it. Perhaps, she knew everything. Or maybe just like Bhura had mentioned to Vikram, she knew about it only in bits and pieces. Nirmala was happy that they were not asking her about it. She would not have told it anyway. There was a chance that the subject would become a sore point in their relationship in the future. The three friends, who knew much more, were not tied with any such promise. And they were more than happy that Nirmala didn't talk about it. They remained in their own silos.

They climbed the stairs talking to each other, much more at comfort than a little while back. Someone from far would have commented that the four friends knew each other from childhood. Behind, the sun was setting down into the Ganges, turning the waters slightly pink in color.

❁ ❁ ❁